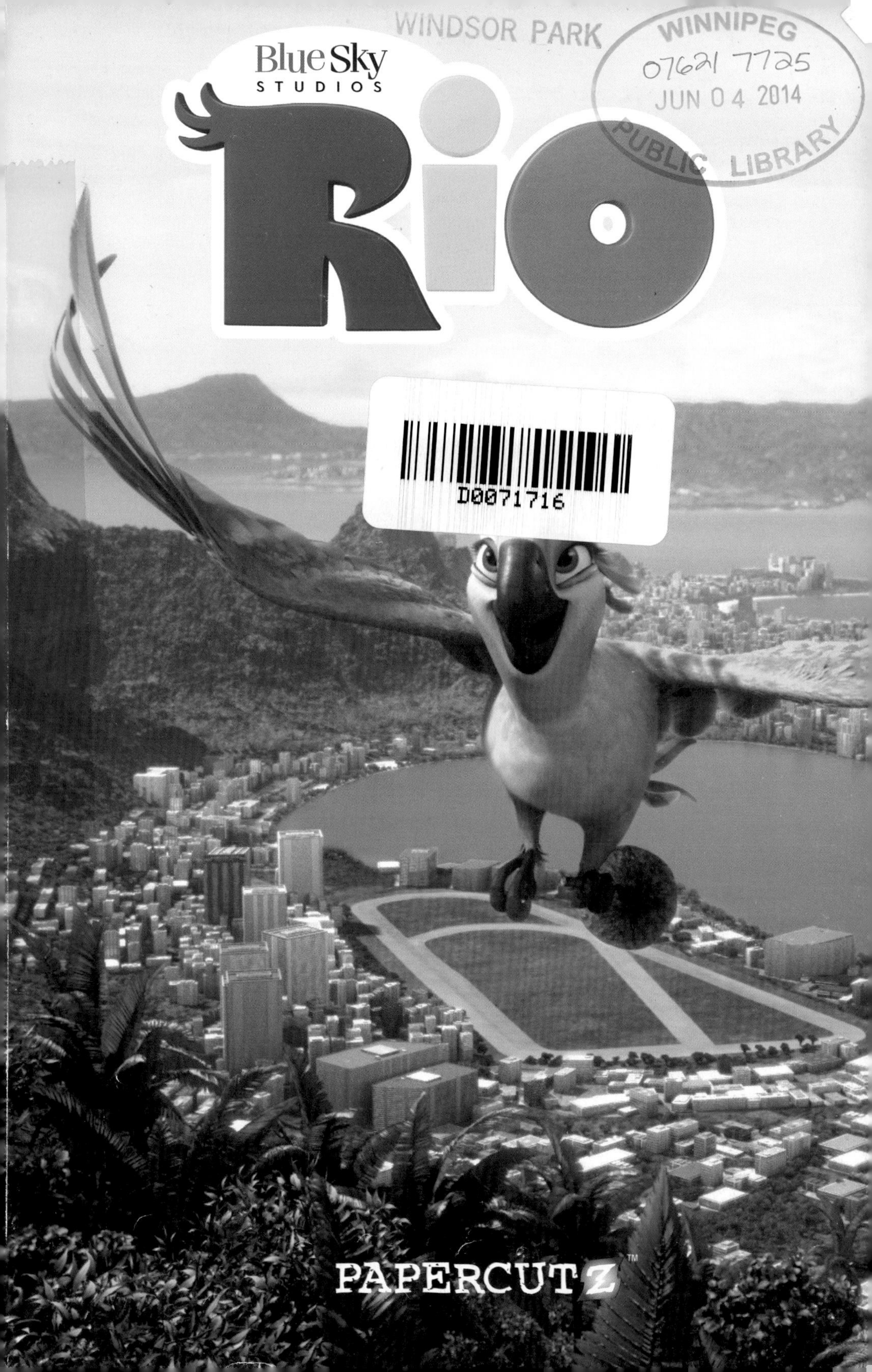
Blue Sky
STUDIOS
Rio
PAPERCUTZ™

Graphic Novels Available From PAPERCUTZ™

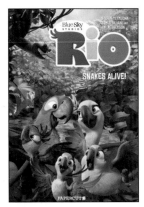

Graphic Novel #1
"Snakes Alive!"

Coming Soon
Graphic Novel #2

Blue Sky STUDIOS

RIO

"SNAKES ALIVE!"

STEFAN PETRUCHA – WRITER

JAMES SILVANI AND

AMY MEBBERSON – ARTISTS

PAPERCUTZ™

New York

RIO
#1 "Snakes Alive!"
Stefan Petrucha – Writer
James Silvani and Amy Mebberson – Artists
Amy Mebberson – Colorist
Tom Orzechowski – Letterer
JayJay Jackson – Bird Doctoring
Dawn K. Guzzo – Production
Beth Scorzato – Production Coordinator
Melanie Bartlett, Alycia Cunningham, John Donkin, Josh Izzo, Benjamin Lapides, Jesse Post, Patrick Skelly, Karen Toliver, Lauren Winarski – Special Thanks
Michael Petranek – Associate Editor
Jim Salicrup
Editor-in-Chief

ISBN: 978-1-59707-507-7 paperback edition
ISBN: 978-1-59707-508-4 hardcover edition

Printed in Canada
March 2014 by Friesens
1 Printers Way
Altona, MB R0G 0B0

Papercutz books may be purchased for business or promotional use.
For information on bulk purchases please contact Macmillan Corporate and Premium Sales Department at (800) 221-7945 x5442.

Distributed by Macmillan
First Printing

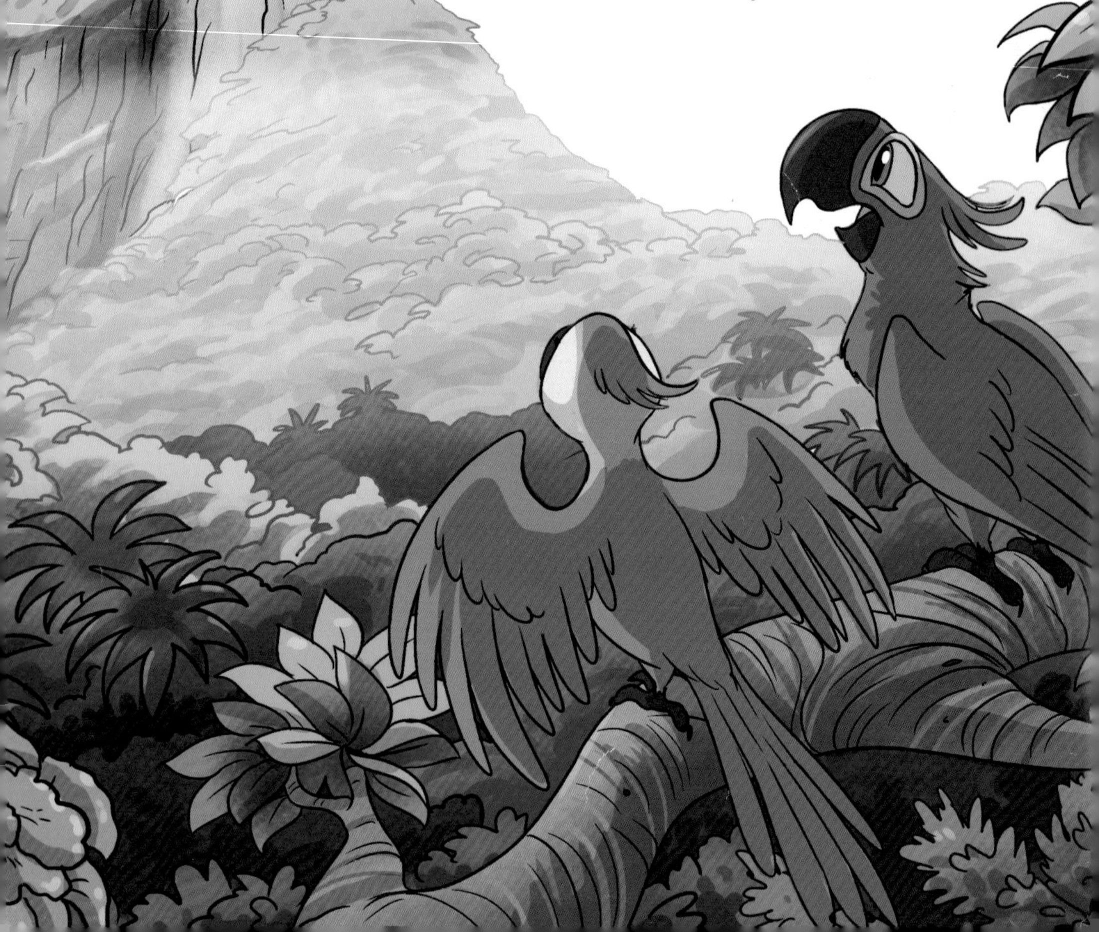

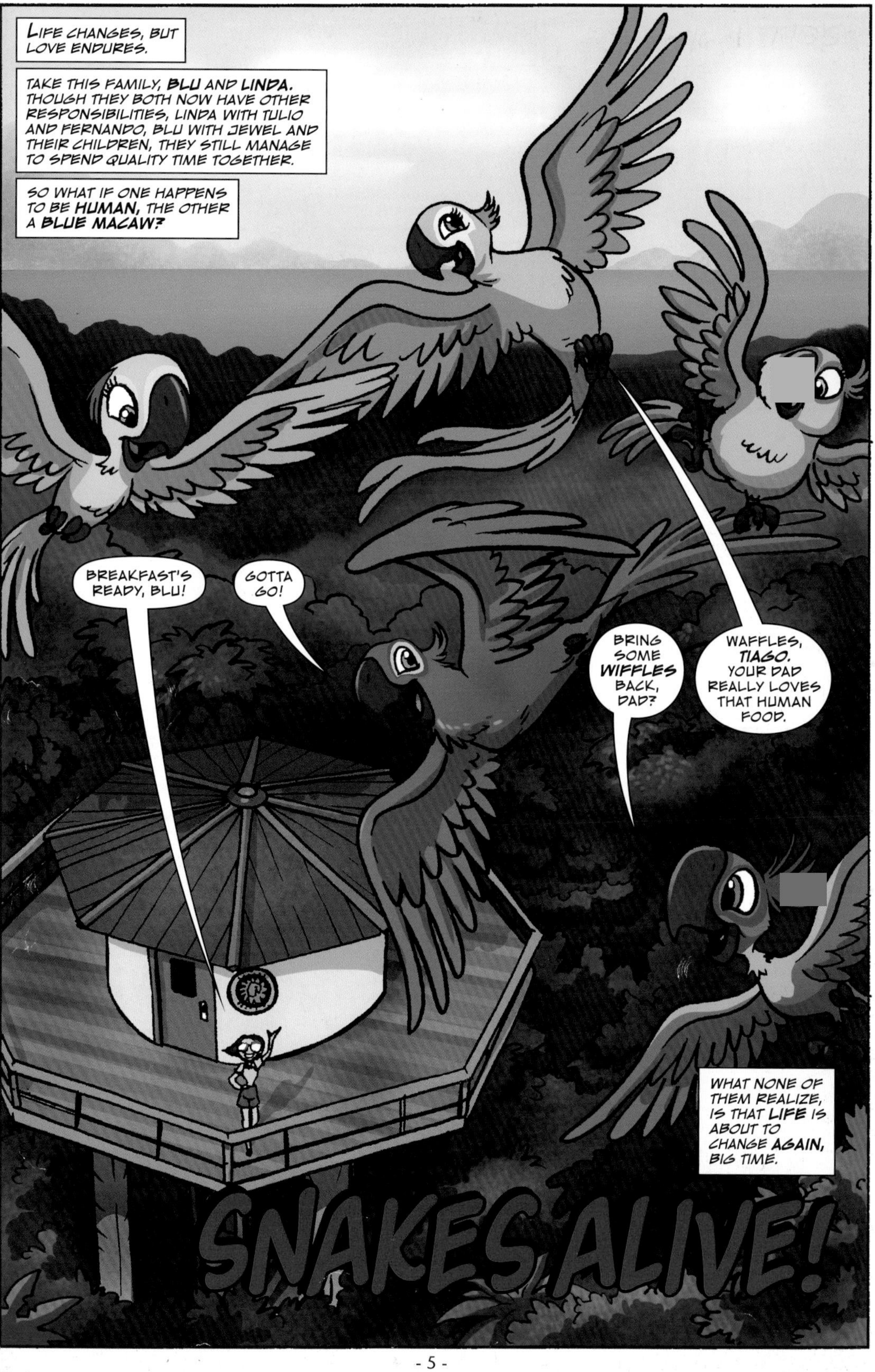
LIFE CHANGES, BUT LOVE ENDURES.
TAKE THIS FAMILY, BLU AND LINDA. THOUGH THEY BOTH NOW HAVE OTHER RESPONSIBILITIES, LINDA WITH TULIO AND FERNANDO, BLU WITH JEWEL AND THEIR CHILDREN, THEY STILL MANAGE TO SPEND QUALITY TIME TOGETHER.
SO WHAT IF ONE HAPPENS TO BE HUMAN, THE OTHER A BLUE MACAW?
BREAKFAST'S READY, BLU!
GOTTA GO!
BRING SOME WIFFLES BACK, DAD?
WAFFLES, TIAGO. YOUR DAD REALLY LOVES THAT HUMAN FOOD.
WHAT NONE OF THEM REALIZE, IS THAT LIFE IS ABOUT TO CHANGE AGAIN, BIG TIME.
SNAKES ALIVE!

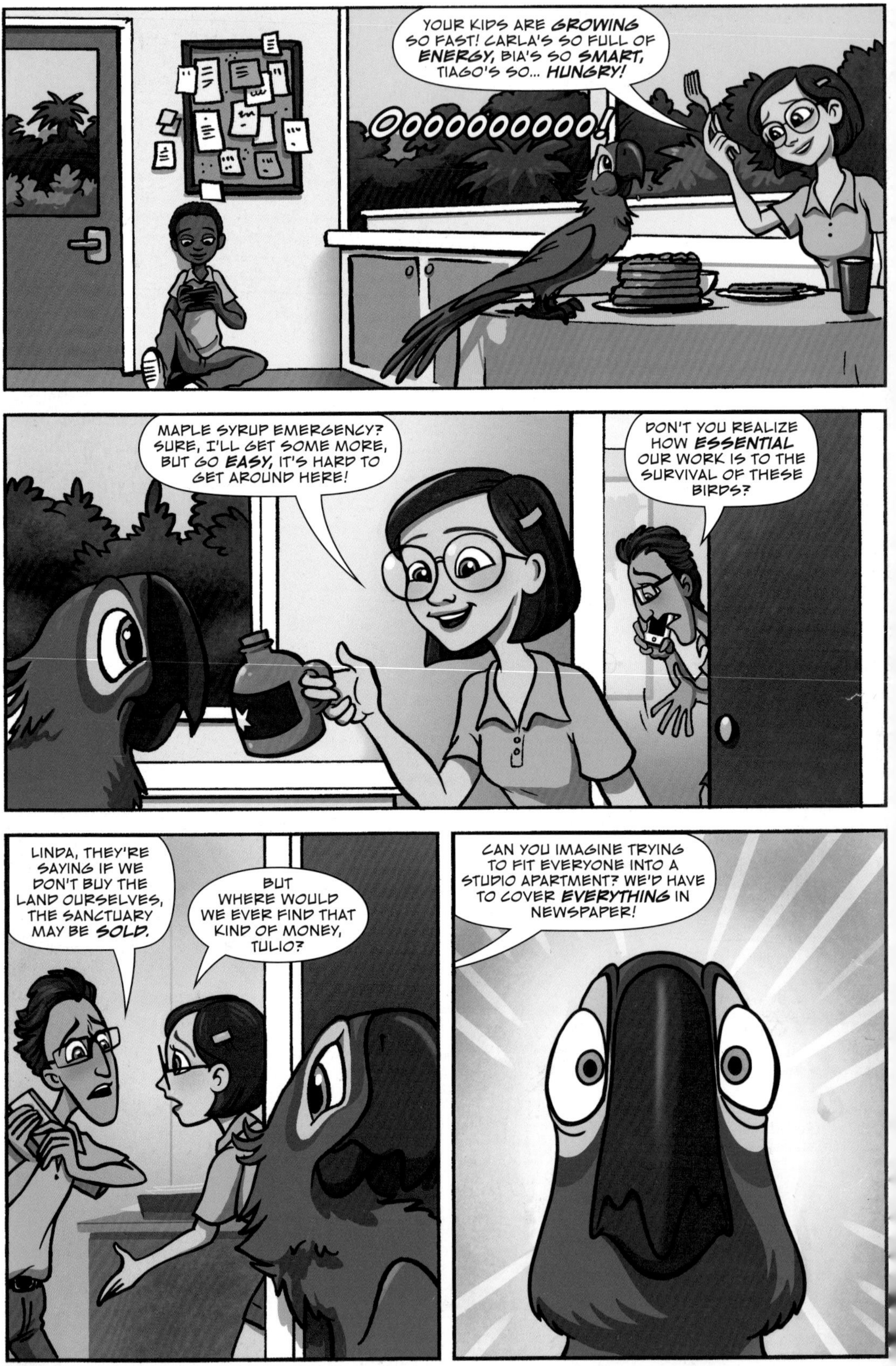
YOUR KIDS ARE GROWING SO FAST! CARLA'S SO FULL OF ENERGY, BIA'S SO SMART, TIAGO'S SO... HUNGRY!
OOOOOOOOOO!
MAPLE SYRUP EMERGENCY? SURE, I'LL GET SOME MORE, BUT GO EASY, IT'S HARD TO GET AROUND HERE!
DON'T YOU REALIZE HOW ESSENTIAL OUR WORK IS TO THE SURVIVAL OF THESE BIRDS?
LINDA, THEY'RE SAYING IF WE DON'T BUY THE LAND OURSELVES, THE SANCTUARY MAY BE SOLD.
BUT WHERE WOULD WE EVER FIND THAT KIND OF MONEY, TULIO?
CAN YOU IMAGINE TRYING TO FIT EVERYONE INTO A STUDIO APARTMENT? WE'D HAVE TO COVER EVERYTHING IN NEWSPAPER!

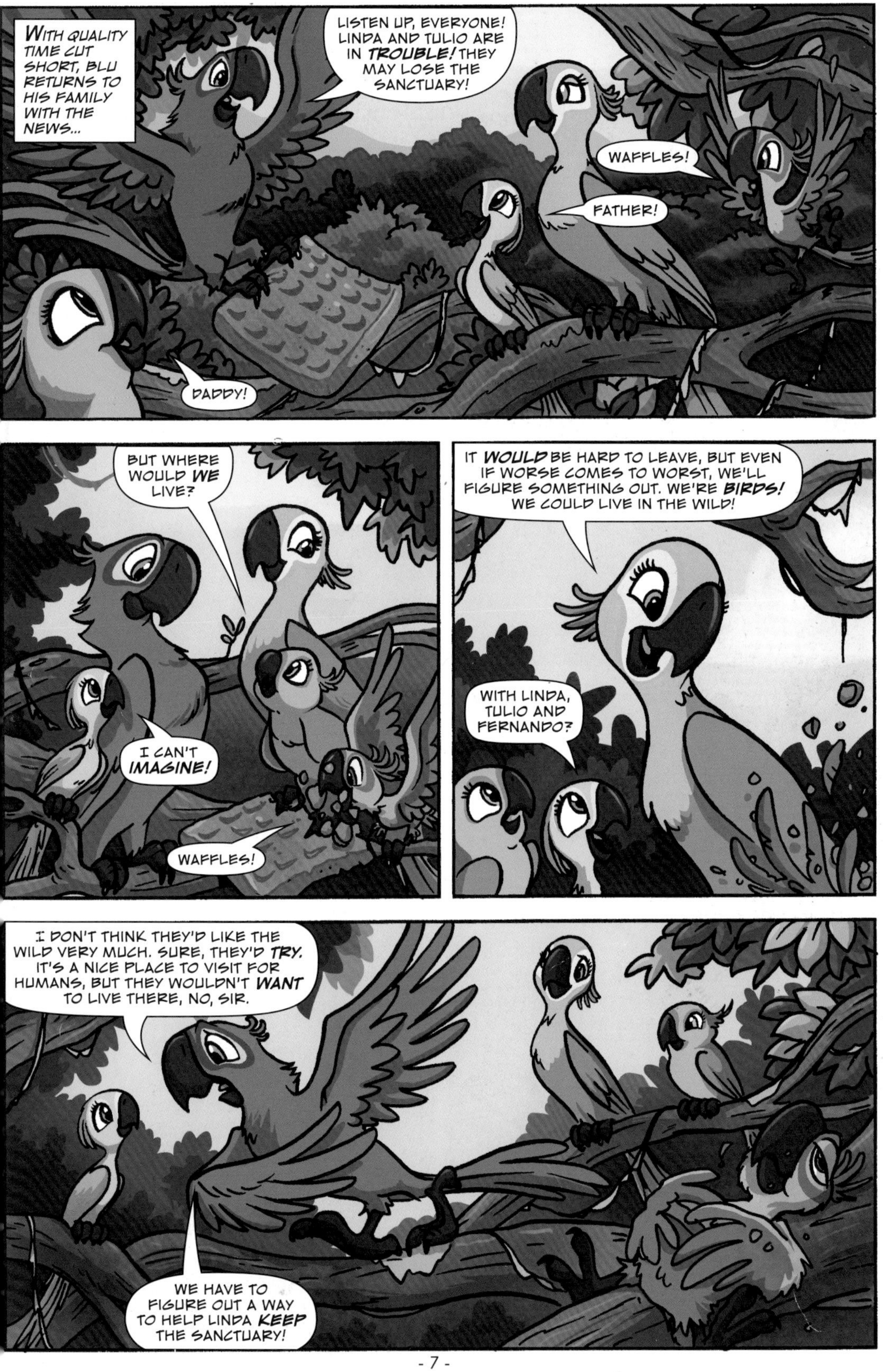

WITH QUALITY TIME CUT SHORT, BLU RETURNS TO HIS FAMILY WITH THE NEWS...
LISTEN UP, EVERYONE! LINDA AND TULIO ARE IN TROUBLE! THEY MAY LOSE THE SANCTUARY!
WAFFLES!
FATHER!
DADDY!
BUT WHERE WOULD WE LIVE?
I CAN'T IMAGINE!
WAFFLES!
IT WOULD BE HARD TO LEAVE, BUT EVEN IF WORSE COMES TO WORST, WE'LL FIGURE SOMETHING OUT. WE'RE BIRDS! WE COULD LIVE IN THE WILD!
WITH LINDA, TULIO AND FERNANDO?
I DON'T THINK THEY'D LIKE THE WILD VERY MUCH. SURE, THEY'D TRY. IT'S A NICE PLACE TO VISIT FOR HUMANS, BUT THEY WOULDN'T WANT TO LIVE THERE, NO, SIR.
WE HAVE TO FIGURE OUT A WAY TO HELP LINDA KEEP THE SANCTUARY!

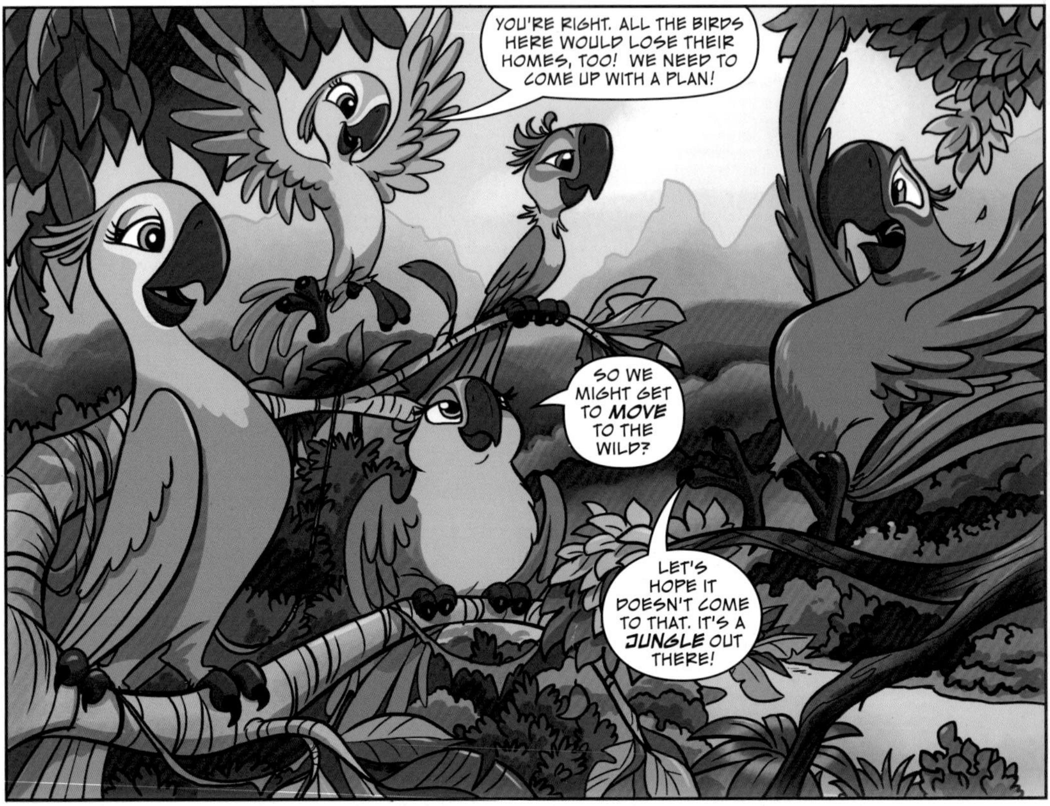
YOU'RE RIGHT. ALL THE BIRDS HERE WOULD LOSE THEIR HOMES, TOO! WE NEED TO COME UP WITH A PLAN!
SO WE MIGHT GET TO **MOVE** TO THE WILD?
LET'S HOPE IT DOESN'T COME TO THAT. IT'S A **JUNGLE** OUT THERE!

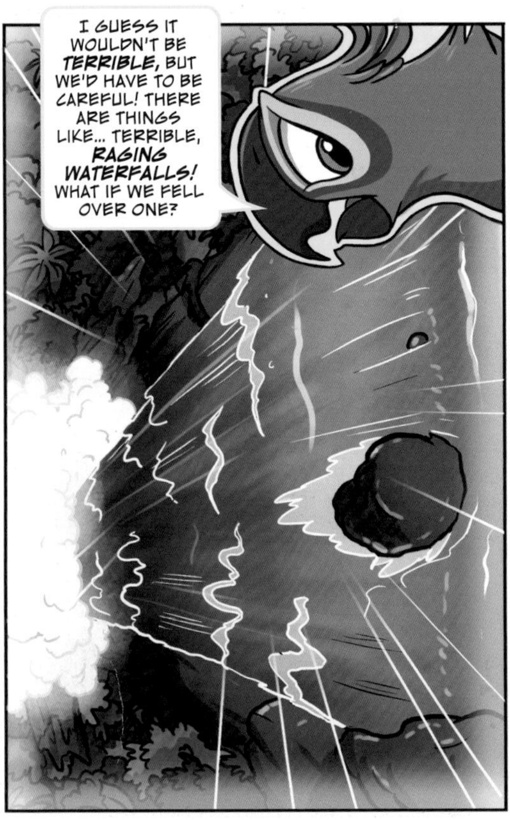
I GUESS IT WOULDN'T BE **TERRIBLE,** BUT WE'D HAVE TO BE CAREFUL! THERE ARE THINGS LIKE... TERRIBLE, **RAGING WATERFALLS!** WHAT IF WE FELL OVER ONE?

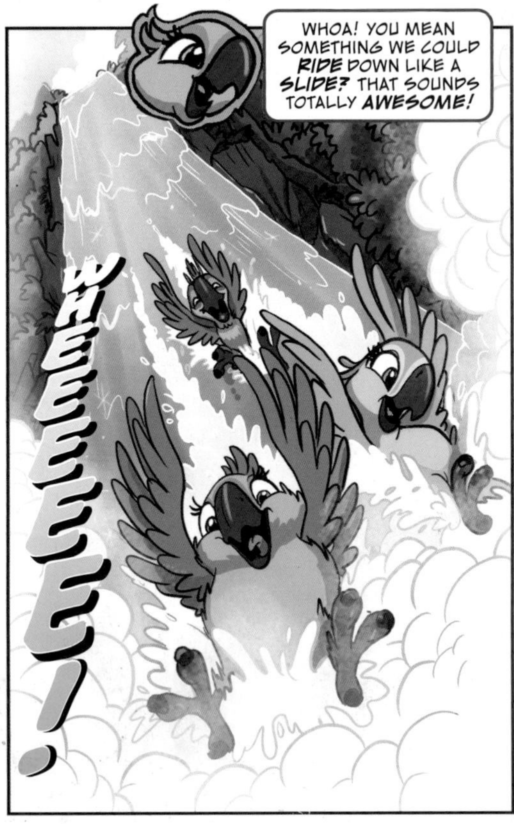
WHOA! YOU MEAN SOMETHING WE COULD **RIDE** DOWN LIKE A **SLIDE?** THAT SOUNDS TOTALLY **AWESOME!**
WHEEEEEE!!

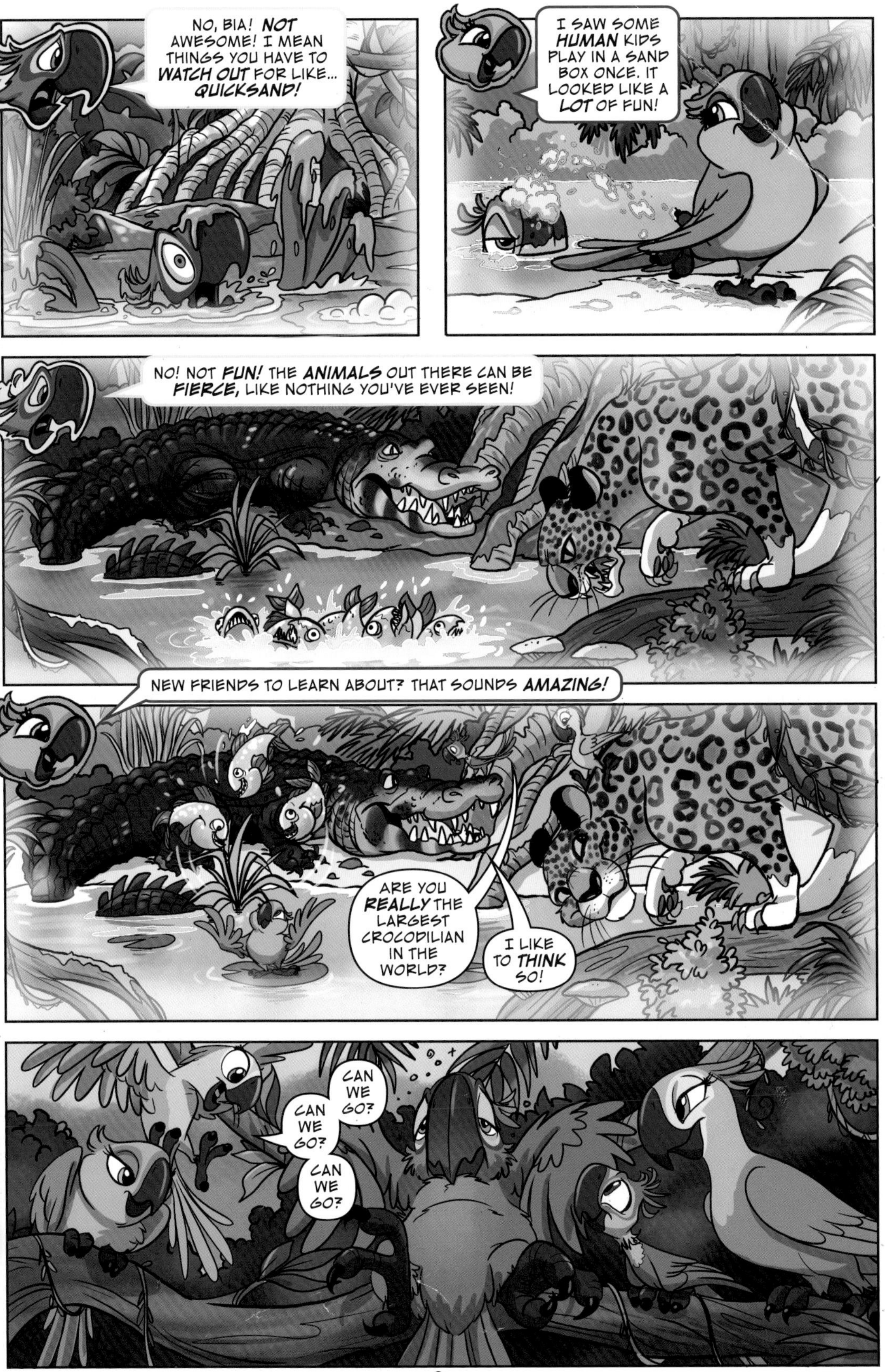
NO, BIA! NOT AWESOME! I MEAN THINGS YOU HAVE TO WATCH OUT FOR LIKE... QUICKSAND!
I SAW SOME HUMAN KIDS PLAY IN A SAND BOX ONCE. IT LOOKED LIKE A LOT OF FUN!
NO! NOT FUN! THE ANIMALS OUT THERE CAN BE FIERCE, LIKE NOTHING YOU'VE EVER SEEN!
NEW FRIENDS TO LEARN ABOUT? THAT SOUNDS AMAZING!
ARE YOU REALLY THE LARGEST CROCODILIAN IN THE WORLD?
I LIKE TO THINK SO!
CAN WE GO?
CAN WE GO?
CAN WE GO?

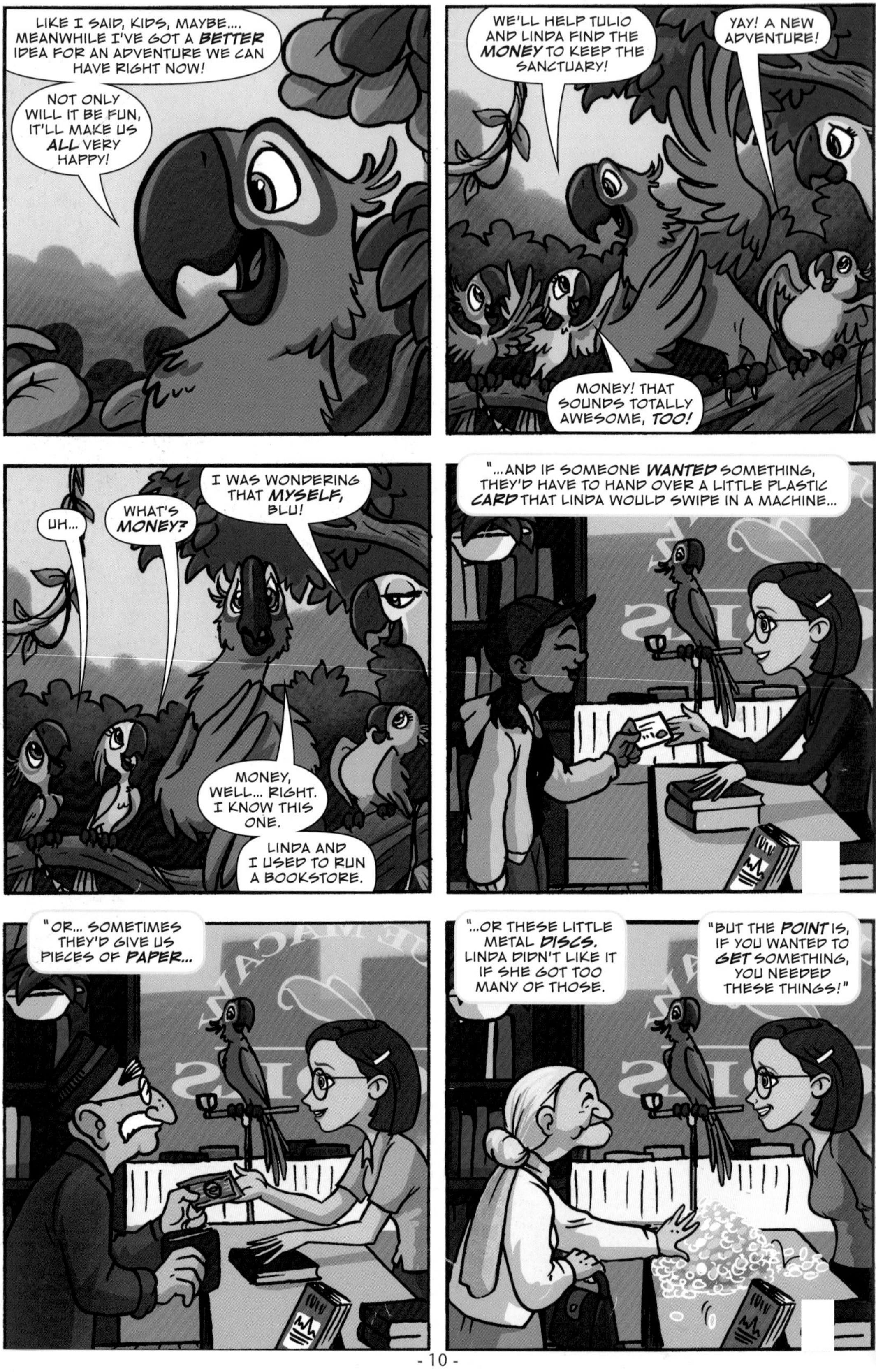
LIKE I SAID, KIDS, MAYBE.... MEANWHILE I'VE GOT A BETTER IDEA FOR AN ADVENTURE WE CAN HAVE RIGHT NOW!
NOT ONLY WILL IT BE FUN, IT'LL MAKE US ALL VERY HAPPY!
WE'LL HELP TULIO AND LINDA FIND THE MONEY TO KEEP THE SANCTUARY!
YAY! A NEW ADVENTURE!
MONEY! THAT SOUNDS TOTALLY AWESOME, TOO!
UH...
WHAT'S MONEY?
I WAS WONDERING THAT MYSELF, BLU!
MONEY, WELL... RIGHT. I KNOW THIS ONE.
LINDA AND I USED TO RUN A BOOKSTORE.
"...AND IF SOMEONE WANTED SOMETHING, THEY'D HAVE TO HAND OVER A LITTLE PLASTIC CARD THAT LINDA WOULD SWIPE IN A MACHINE...
"OR... SOMETIMES THEY'D GIVE US PIECES OF PAPER...
"...OR THESE LITTLE METAL DISCS. LINDA DIDN'T LIKE IT IF SHE GOT TOO MANY OF THOSE.
"BUT THE POINT IS, IF YOU WANTED TO GET SOMETHING, YOU NEEDED THESE THINGS!"

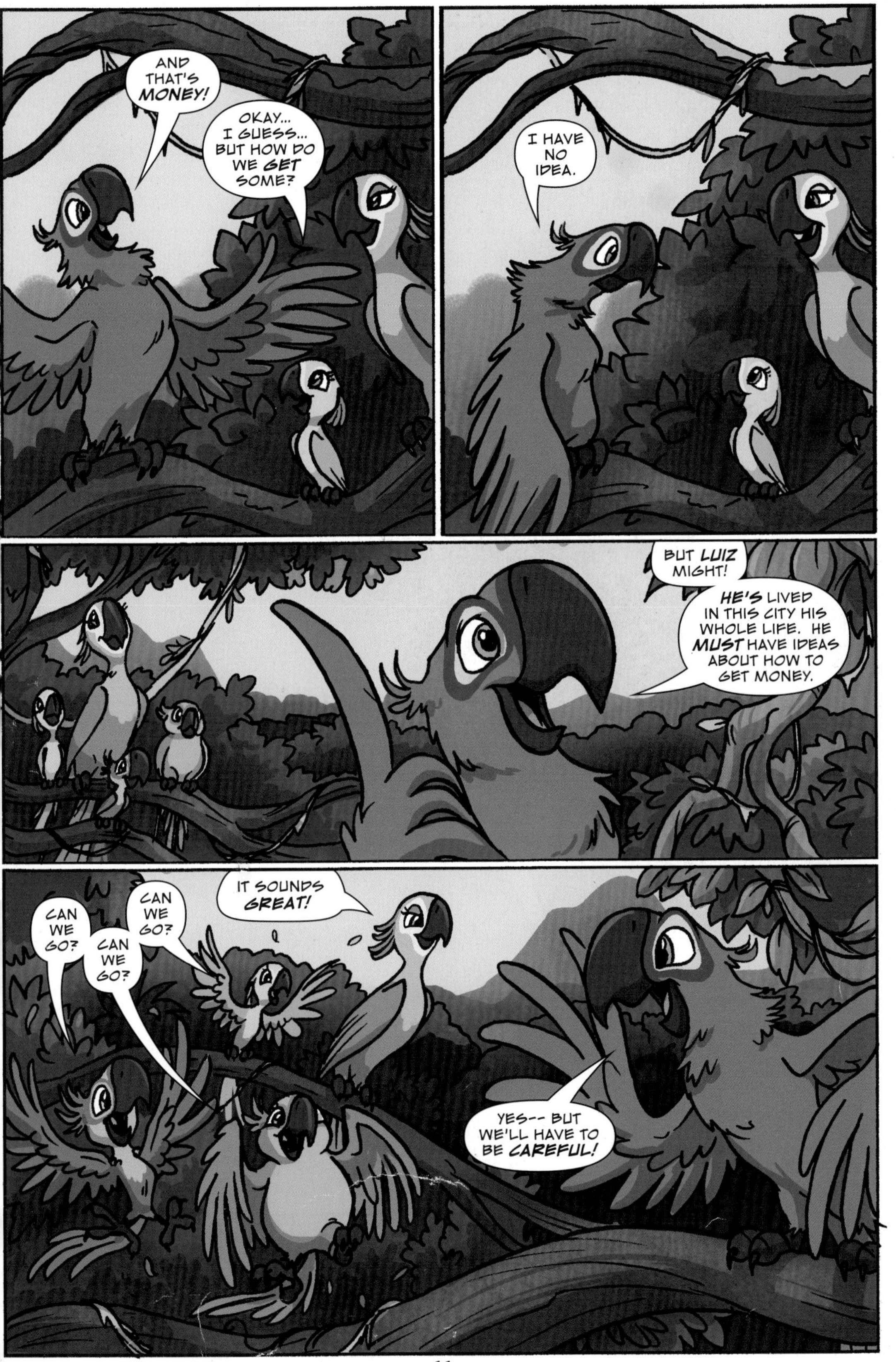
AND THAT'S MONEY!
OKAY... I GUESS... BUT HOW DO WE GET SOME?
I HAVE NO IDEA.
BUT LUIZ MIGHT!
HE'S LIVED IN THIS CITY HIS WHOLE LIFE. HE MUST HAVE IDEAS ABOUT HOW TO GET MONEY.
CAN WE GO?
CAN WE GO?
CAN WE GO?
IT SOUNDS GREAT!
YES-- BUT WE'LL HAVE TO BE CAREFUL!

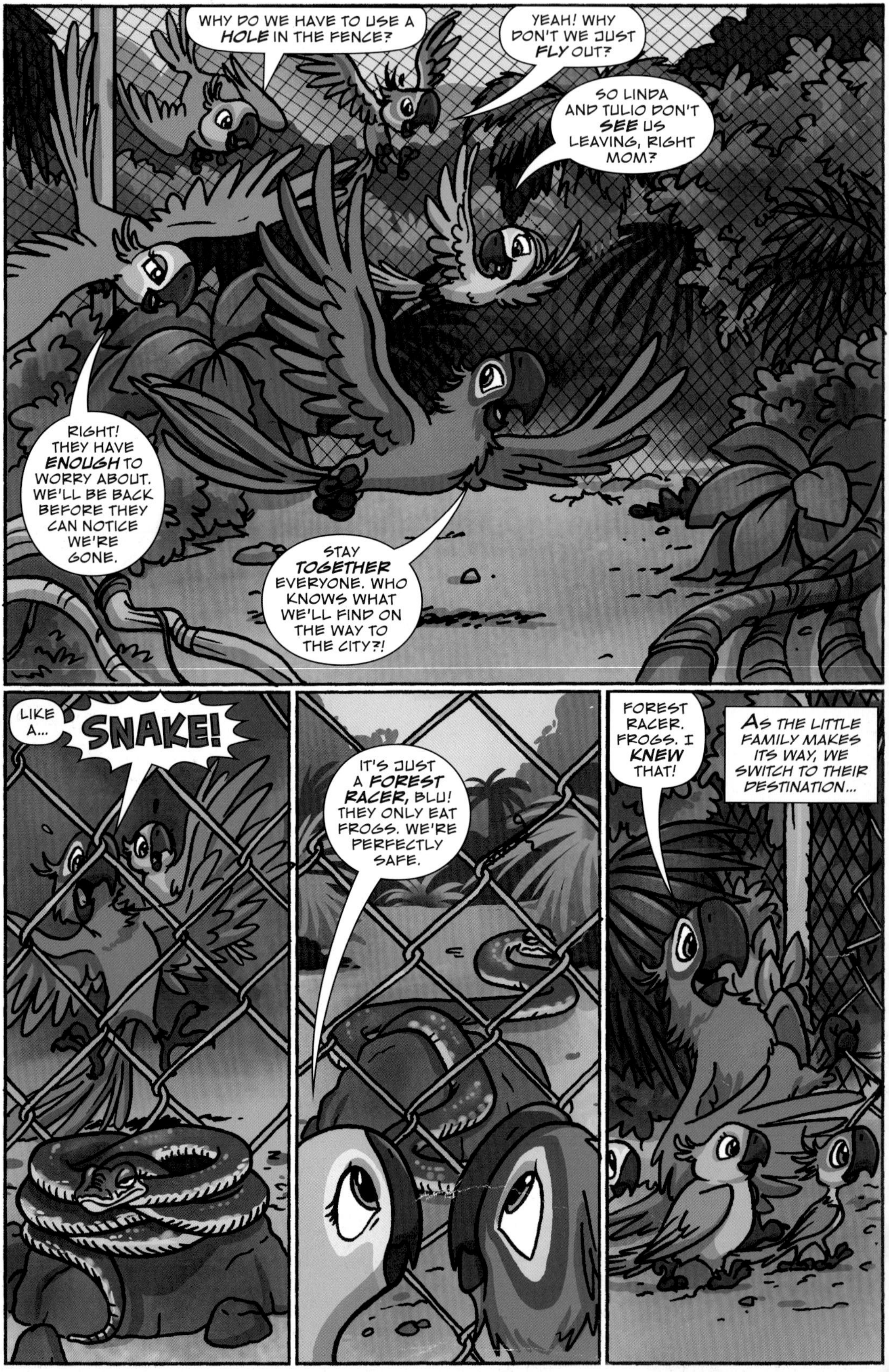
WHY DO WE HAVE TO USE A HOLE IN THE FENCE?
YEAH! WHY DON'T WE JUST FLY OUT?
SO LINDA AND TULIO DON'T SEE US LEAVING, RIGHT MOM?
RIGHT! THEY HAVE ENOUGH TO WORRY ABOUT. WE'LL BE BACK BEFORE THEY CAN NOTICE WE'RE GONE.
STAY TOGETHER EVERYONE. WHO KNOWS WHAT WE'LL FIND ON THE WAY TO THE CITY?!
LIKE A...
SNAKE!
IT'S JUST A FOREST RACER, BLU! THEY ONLY EAT FROGS. WE'RE PERFECTLY SAFE.
FOREST RACER. FROGS. I KNEW THAT!
AS THE LITTLE FAMILY MAKES ITS WAY, WE SWITCH TO THEIR DESTINATION...

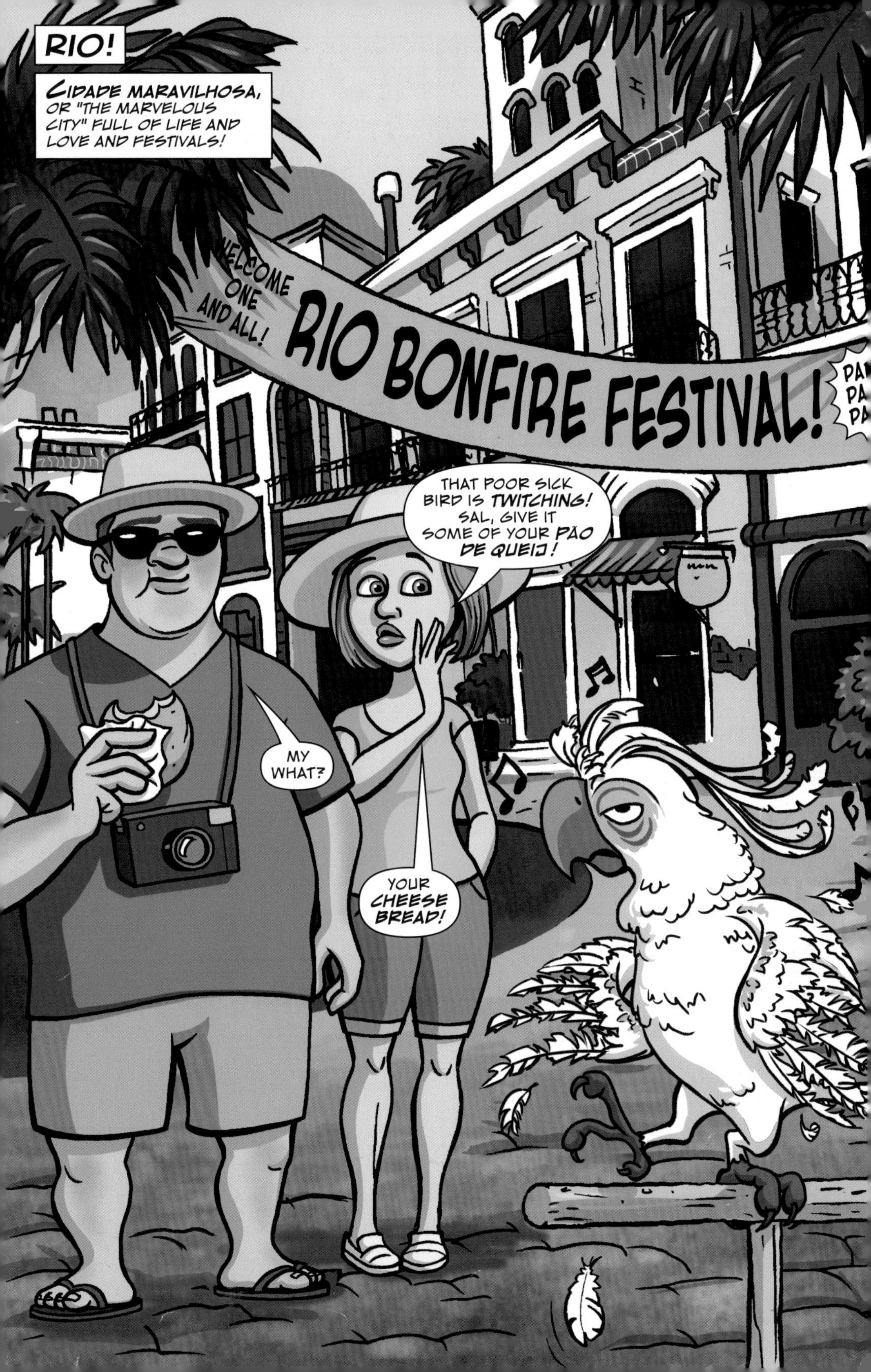
RIO!
CIDADE MARAVILHOSA, OR "THE MARVELOUS CITY" FULL OF LIFE AND LOVE AND FESTIVALS!
WELCOME ONE AND ALL! RIO BONFIRE FESTIVAL!
THAT POOR SICK BIRD IS TWITCHING! SAL, GIVE IT SOME OF YOUR PÃO DE QUEIJ!
MY WHAT?
YOUR CHEESE BREAD!

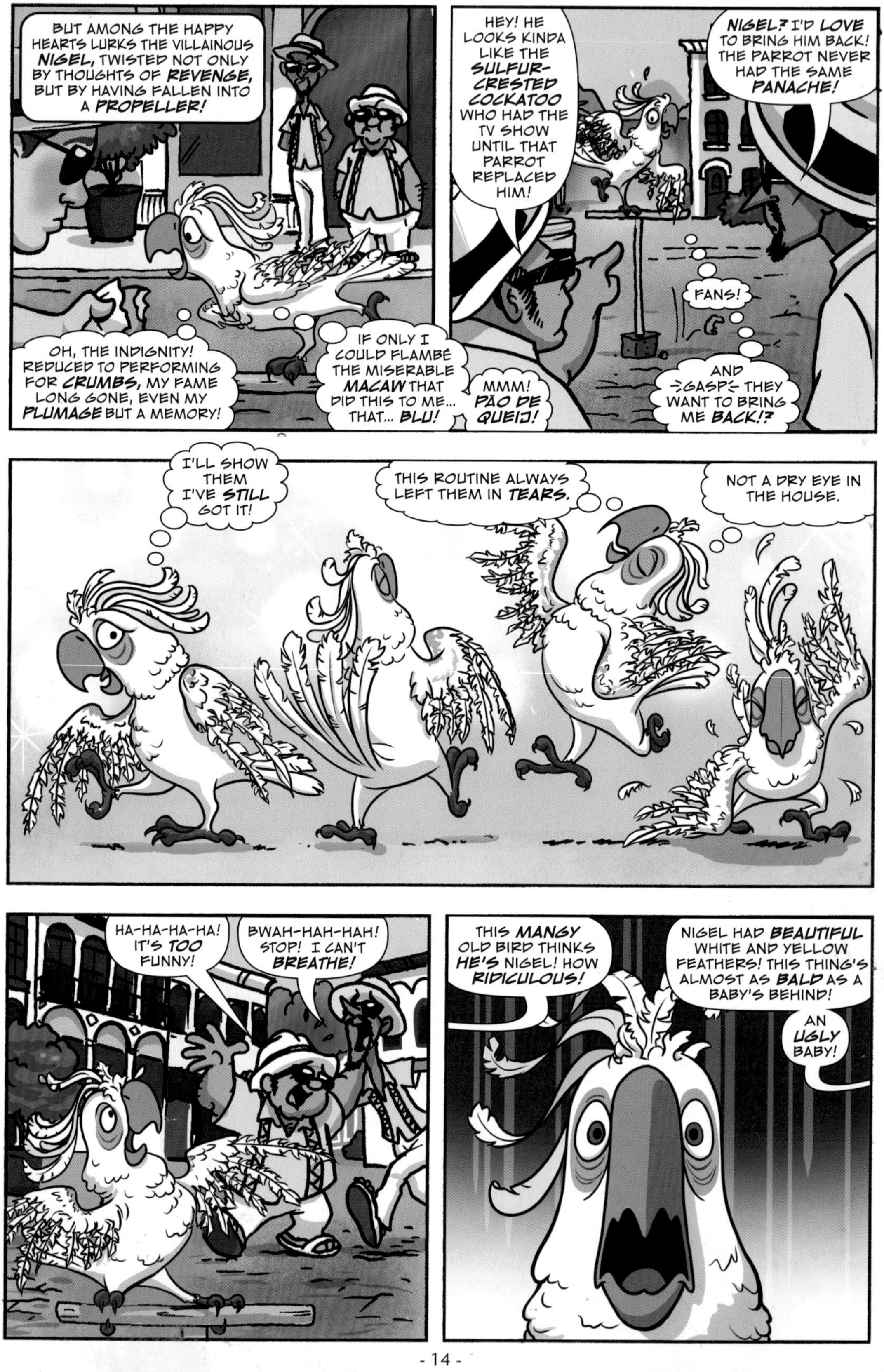
BUT AMONG THE HAPPY HEARTS LURKS THE VILLAINOUS NIGEL, TWISTED NOT ONLY BY THOUGHTS OF REVENGE, BUT BY HAVING FALLEN INTO A PROPELLER!
OH, THE INDIGNITY! REDUCED TO PERFORMING FOR CRUMBS, MY FAME LONG GONE, EVEN MY PLUMAGE BUT A MEMORY!
IF ONLY I COULD FLAMBÉ THE MISERABLE MACAW THAT DID THIS TO ME... THAT... BLU!
MMM! PÃO DE QUEIJ!
HEY! HE LOOKS KINDA LIKE THE SULFUR-CRESTED COCKATOO WHO HAD THE TV SHOW UNTIL THAT PARROT REPLACED HIM!
NIGEL? I'D LOVE TO BRING HIM BACK! THE PARROT NEVER HAD THE SAME PANACHE!
FANS!
AND -GASP- THEY WANT TO BRING ME BACK!?
I'LL SHOW THEM I'VE STILL GOT IT!
THIS ROUTINE ALWAYS LEFT THEM IN TEARS.
NOT A DRY EYE IN THE HOUSE.
HA-HA-HA-HA! IT'S TOO FUNNY!
BWAH-HAH-HAH! STOP! I CAN'T BREATHE!
THIS MANGY OLD BIRD THINKS HE'S NIGEL! HOW RIDICULOUS!
NIGEL HAD BEAUTIFUL WHITE AND YELLOW FEATHERS! THIS THING'S ALMOST AS BALD AS A BABY'S BEHIND!
AN UGLY BABY!

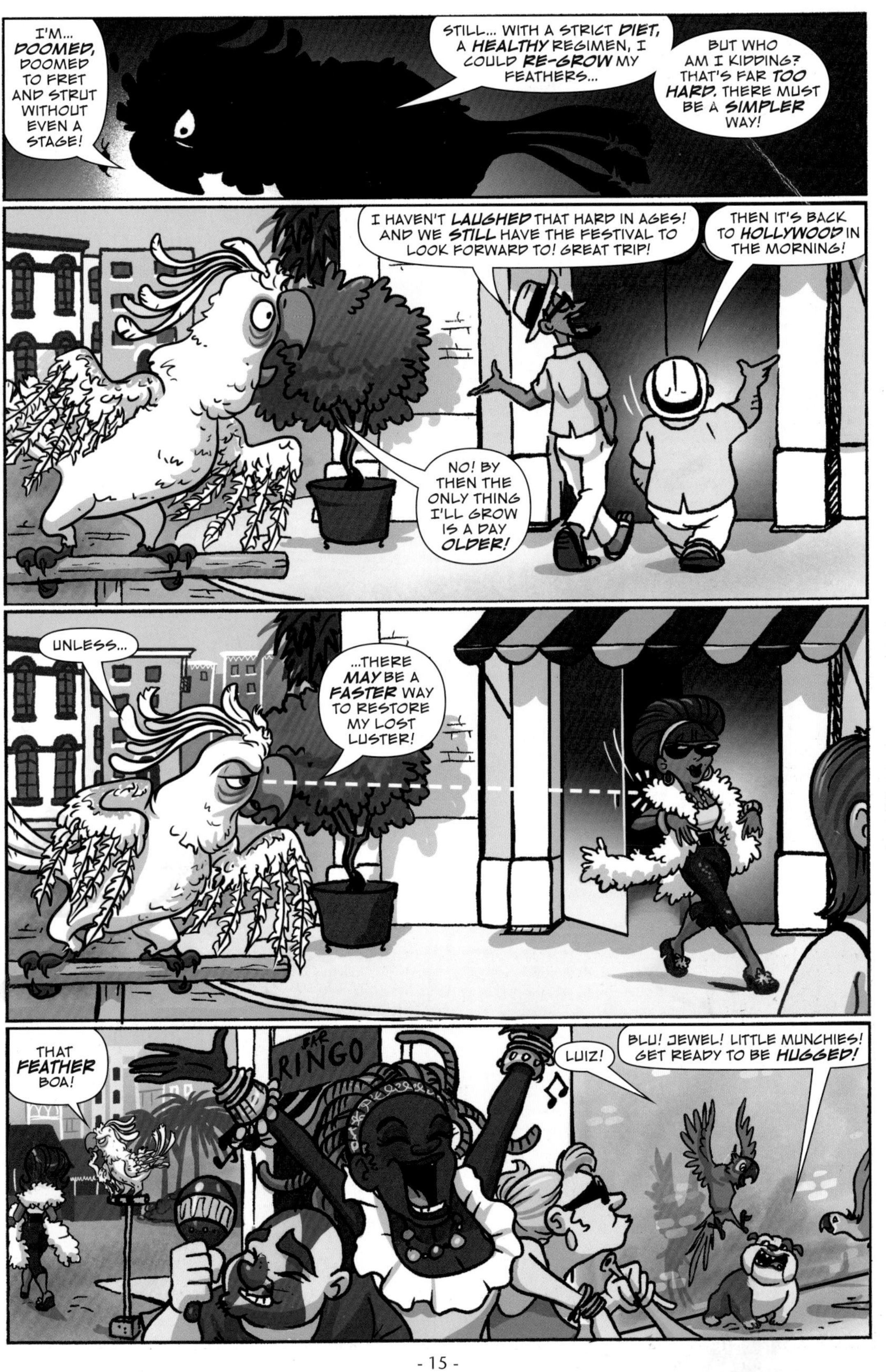
I'M... DOOMED, DOOMED TO FRET AND STRUT WITHOUT EVEN A STAGE!
STILL... WITH A STRICT DIET, A HEALTHY REGIMEN, I COULD RE-GROW MY FEATHERS...
BUT WHO AM I KIDDING? THAT'S FAR TOO HARD. THERE MUST BE A SIMPLER WAY!
I HAVEN'T LAUGHED THAT HARD IN AGES! AND WE STILL HAVE THE FESTIVAL TO LOOK FORWARD TO! GREAT TRIP!
THEN IT'S BACK TO HOLLYWOOD IN THE MORNING!
NO! BY THEN THE ONLY THING I'LL GROW IS A DAY OLDER!
UNLESS...
...THERE MAY BE A FASTER WAY TO RESTORE MY LOST LUSTER!
THAT FEATHER BOA!
RINGO
LUIZ!
BLU! JEWEL! LITTLE MUNCHIES! GET READY TO BE HUGGED!

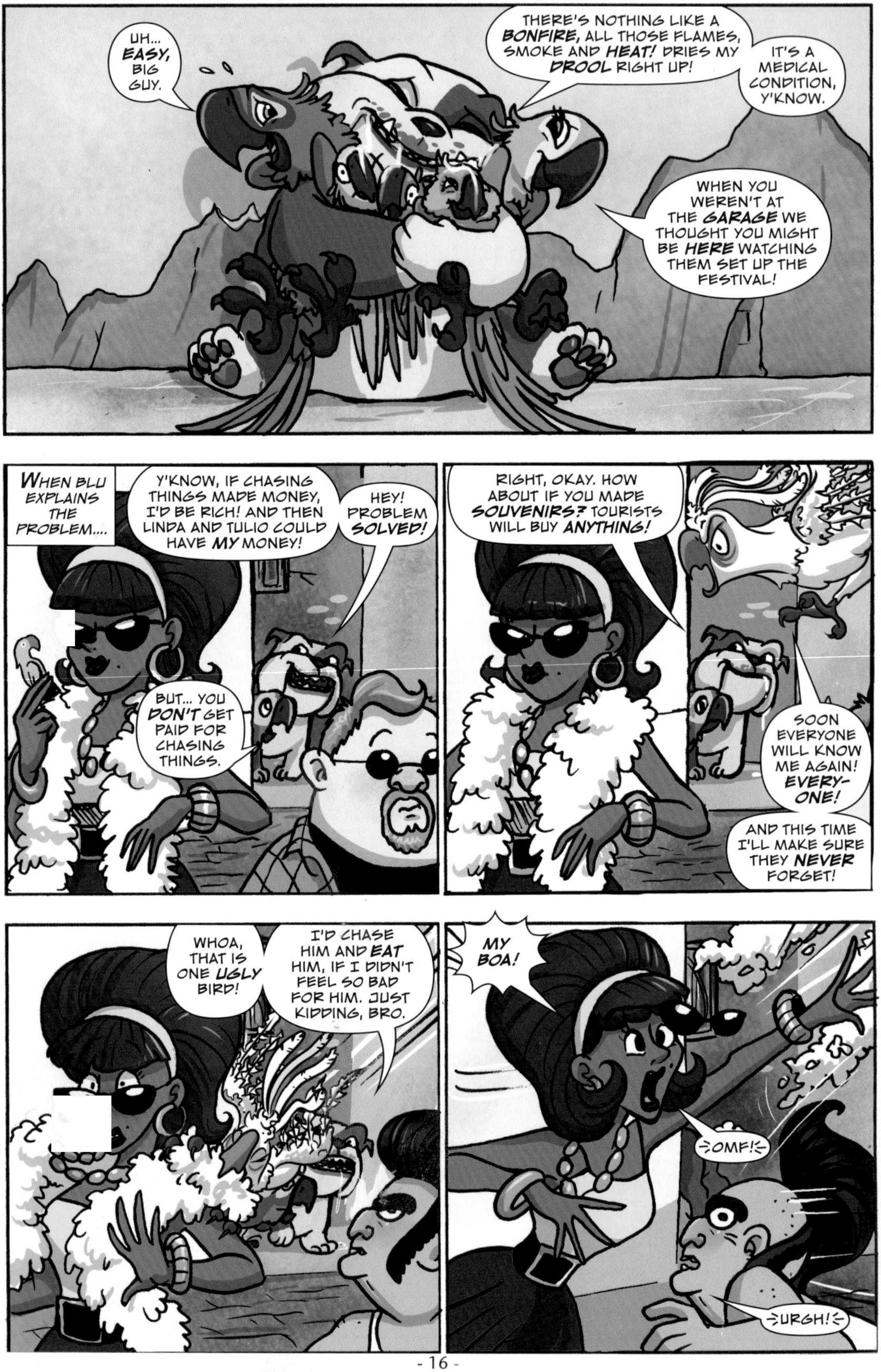
UH... EASY, BIG GUY.
THERE'S NOTHING LIKE A BONFIRE, ALL THOSE FLAMES, SMOKE AND HEAT! DRIES MY DROOL RIGHT UP!
IT'S A MEDICAL CONDITION, Y'KNOW.
WHEN YOU WEREN'T AT THE GARAGE WE THOUGHT YOU MIGHT BE HERE WATCHING THEM SET UP THE FESTIVAL!
WHEN BLU EXPLAINS THE PROBLEM....
Y'KNOW, IF CHASING THINGS MADE MONEY, I'D BE RICH! AND THEN LINDA AND TULIO COULD HAVE MY MONEY!
HEY! PROBLEM SOLVED!
BUT... YOU DON'T GET PAID FOR CHASING THINGS.
RIGHT, OKAY. HOW ABOUT IF YOU MADE SOUVENIRS? TOURISTS WILL BUY ANYTHING!
SOON EVERYONE WILL KNOW ME AGAIN! EVERY-ONE!
AND THIS TIME I'LL MAKE SURE THEY NEVER FORGET!
WHOA, THAT IS ONE UGLY BIRD!
I'D CHASE HIM AND EAT HIM, IF I DIDN'T FEEL SO BAD FOR HIM. JUST KIDDING, BRO.
MY BOA!
OMF!
URGH!

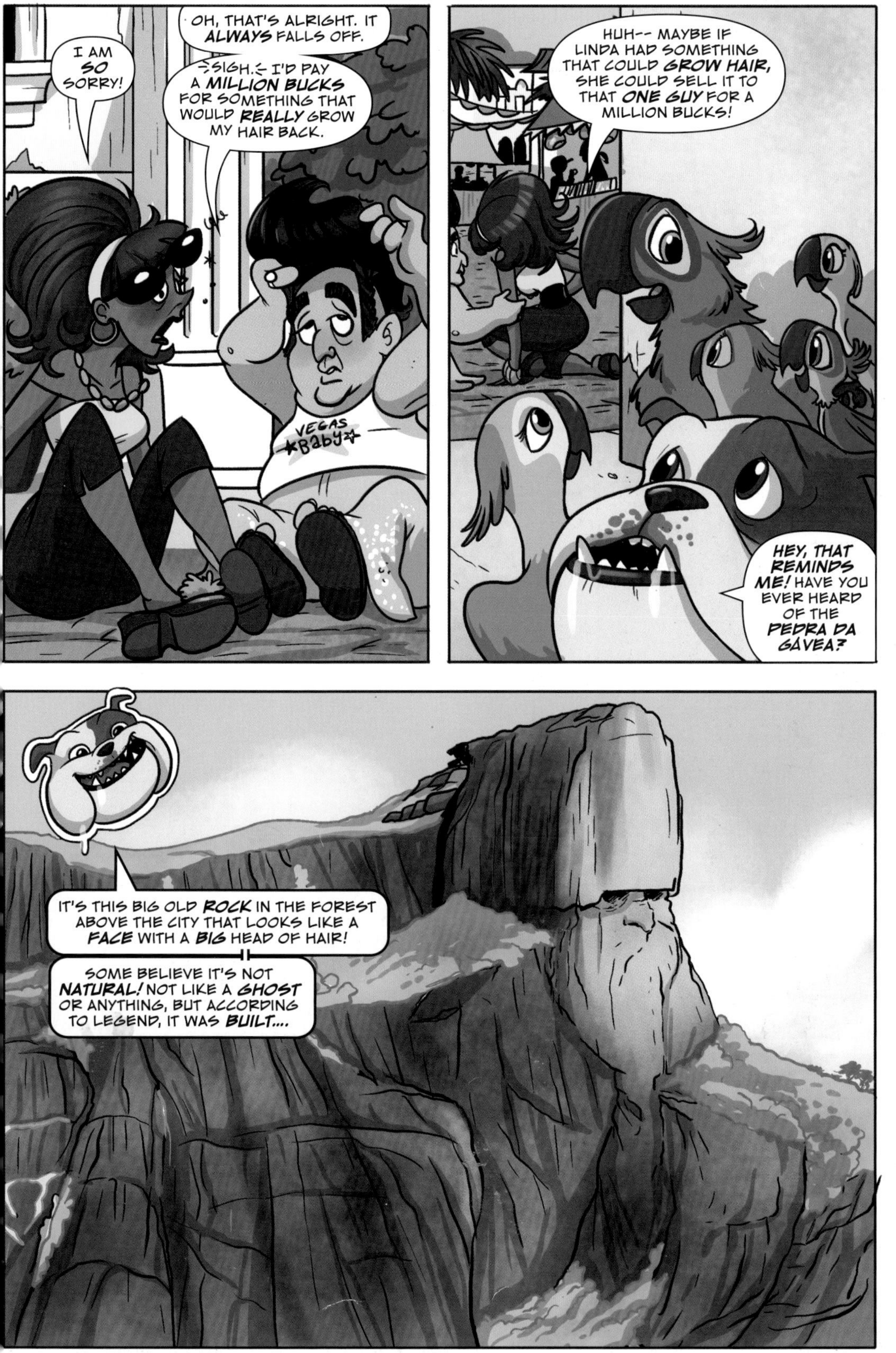
I AM SO SORRY!
OH, THAT'S ALRIGHT. IT ALWAYS FALLS OFF.
⇉SIGH.⇇ I'D PAY A MILLION BUCKS FOR SOMETHING THAT WOULD REALLY GROW MY HAIR BACK.
VEGAS Baby
HUH-- MAYBE IF LINDA HAD SOMETHING THAT COULD GROW HAIR, SHE COULD SELL IT TO THAT ONE GUY FOR A MILLION BUCKS!
HEY, THAT REMINDS ME! HAVE YOU EVER HEARD OF THE PEDRA DA GÁVEA?
IT'S THIS BIG OLD ROCK IN THE FOREST ABOVE THE CITY THAT LOOKS LIKE A FACE WITH A BIG HEAD OF HAIR!
SOME BELIEVE IT'S NOT NATURAL! NOT LIKE A GHOST OR ANYTHING, BUT ACCORDING TO LEGEND, IT WAS BUILT....

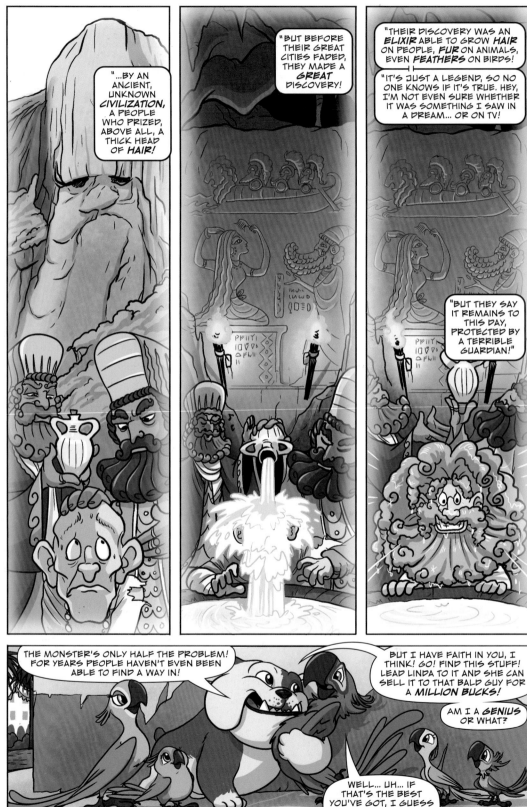

"...BY AN ANCIENT, UNKNOWN *CIVILIZATION*, A PEOPLE WHO PRIZED, ABOVE ALL, A THICK HEAD OF *HAIR!*

"BUT BEFORE THEIR GREAT CITIES FADED, THEY MADE A *GREAT* DISCOVERY!

"THEIR DISCOVERY WAS AN *ELIXIR* ABLE TO GROW *HAIR* ON PEOPLE, *FUR* ON ANIMALS, EVEN *FEATHERS* ON BIRDS!

"IT'S JUST A LEGEND, SO NO ONE KNOWS IF IT'S TRUE. HEY, I'M NOT EVEN SURE WHETHER IT WAS SOMETHING I SAW IN A DREAM... OR ON TV!

"BUT THEY SAY IT REMAINS TO THIS DAY, PROTECTED BY A TERRIBLE GUARDIAN!"

THE MONSTER'S ONLY HALF THE PROBLEM! FOR YEARS PEOPLE HAVEN'T EVEN BEEN ABLE TO FIND A WAY IN!

BUT I HAVE FAITH IN YOU, I THINK! GO! FIND THIS STUFF! LEAD LINDA TO IT AND SHE CAN SELL IT TO THAT BALD GUY FOR A *MILLION BUCKS!*

AM I A *GENIUS* OR WHAT?

WELL... UH... IF THAT'S THE BEST YOU'VE GOT, I GUESS IT'S WORTH A *SHOT.*

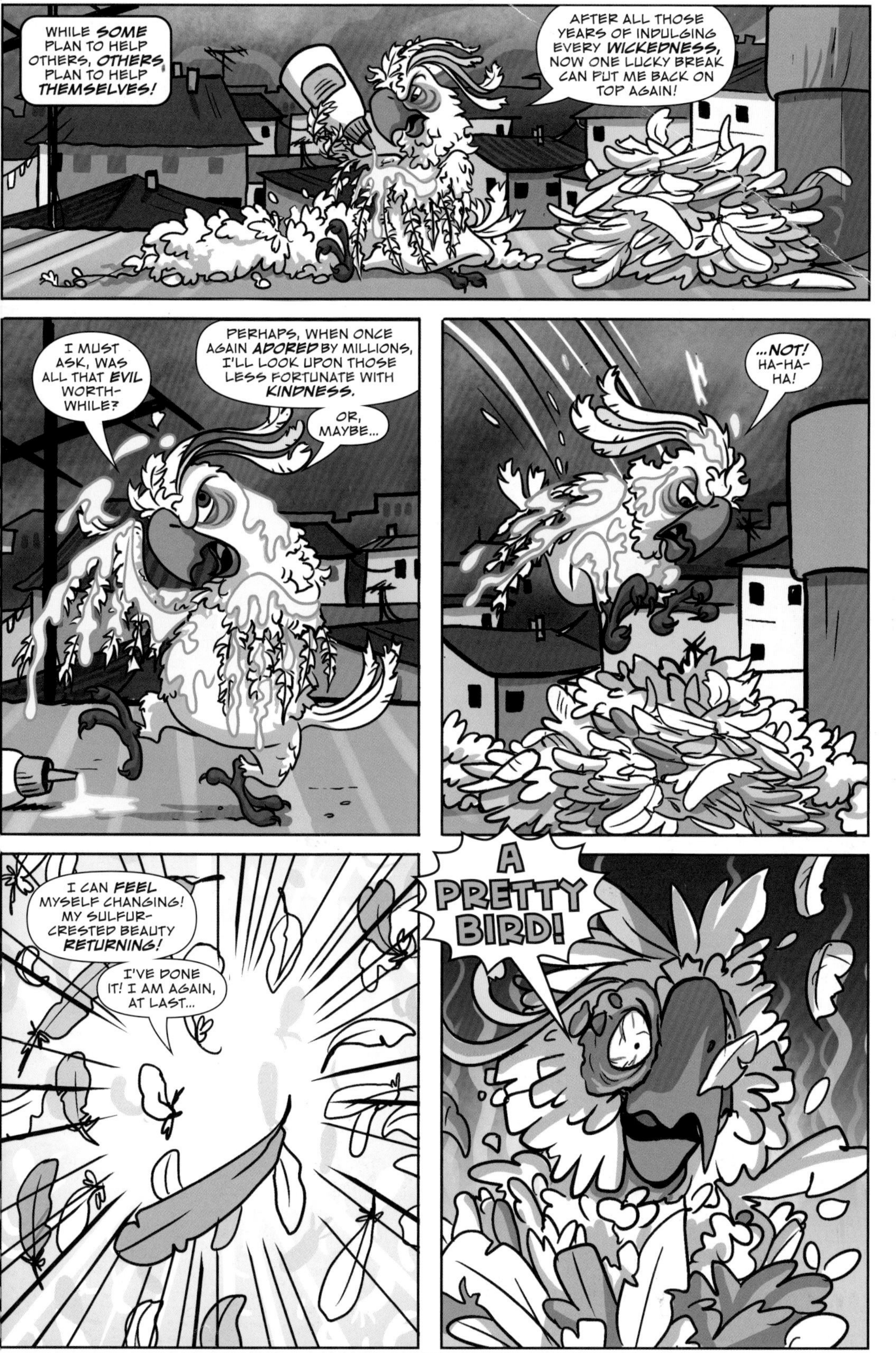
WHILE SOME PLAN TO HELP OTHERS, OTHERS PLAN TO HELP THEMSELVES!
AFTER ALL THOSE YEARS OF INDULGING EVERY WICKEDNESS, NOW ONE LUCKY BREAK CAN PUT ME BACK ON TOP AGAIN!
I MUST ASK, WAS ALL THAT EVIL WORTH-WHILE?
PERHAPS, WHEN ONCE AGAIN ADORED BY MILLIONS, I'LL LOOK UPON THOSE LESS FORTUNATE WITH KINDNESS.
OR, MAYBE...
...NOT! HA-HA-HA!
I CAN FEEL MYSELF CHANGING! MY SULFUR-CRESTED BEAUTY RETURNING!
I'VE DONE IT! I AM AGAIN, AT LAST...
A PRETTY BIRD!

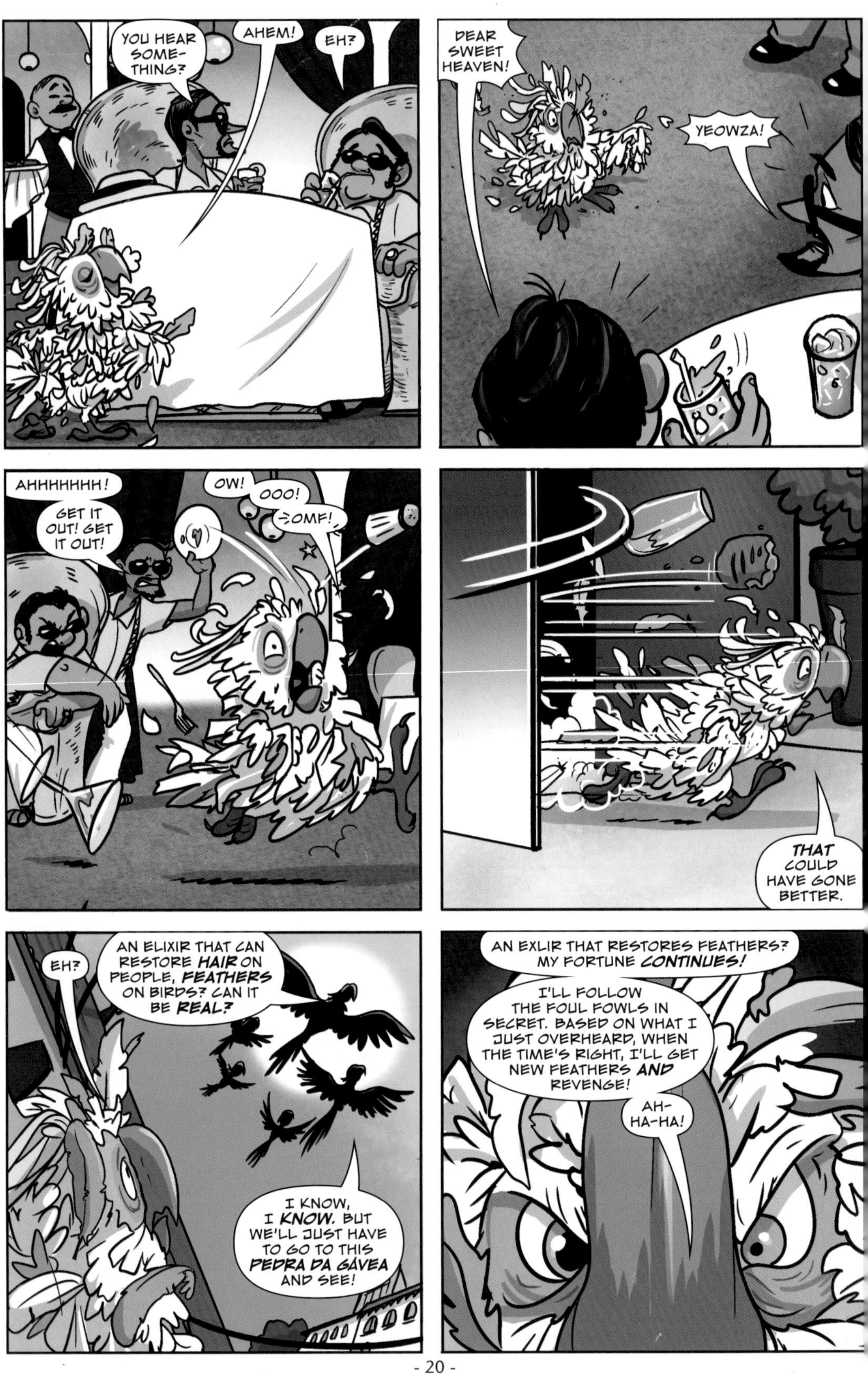

YOU HEAR SOMETHING?
AHEM!
EH?
DEAR SWEET HEAVEN!
YEOWZA!
AHHHHHHH!
GET IT OUT! GET IT OUT!
OW!
OOO!
OMF!
THAT COULD HAVE GONE BETTER.
EH?
AN ELIXIR THAT CAN RESTORE HAIR ON PEOPLE, FEATHERS ON BIRDS? CAN IT BE REAL?
I KNOW, I KNOW. BUT WE'LL JUST HAVE TO GO TO THIS PEDRA DA GÁVEA AND SEE!
AN EXLIR THAT RESTORES FEATHERS? MY FORTUNE CONTINUES!
I'LL FOLLOW THE FOUL FOWLS IN SECRET. BASED ON WHAT I JUST OVERHEARD, WHEN THE TIME'S RIGHT, I'LL GET NEW FEATHERS AND REVENGE!
AH-HA-HA!

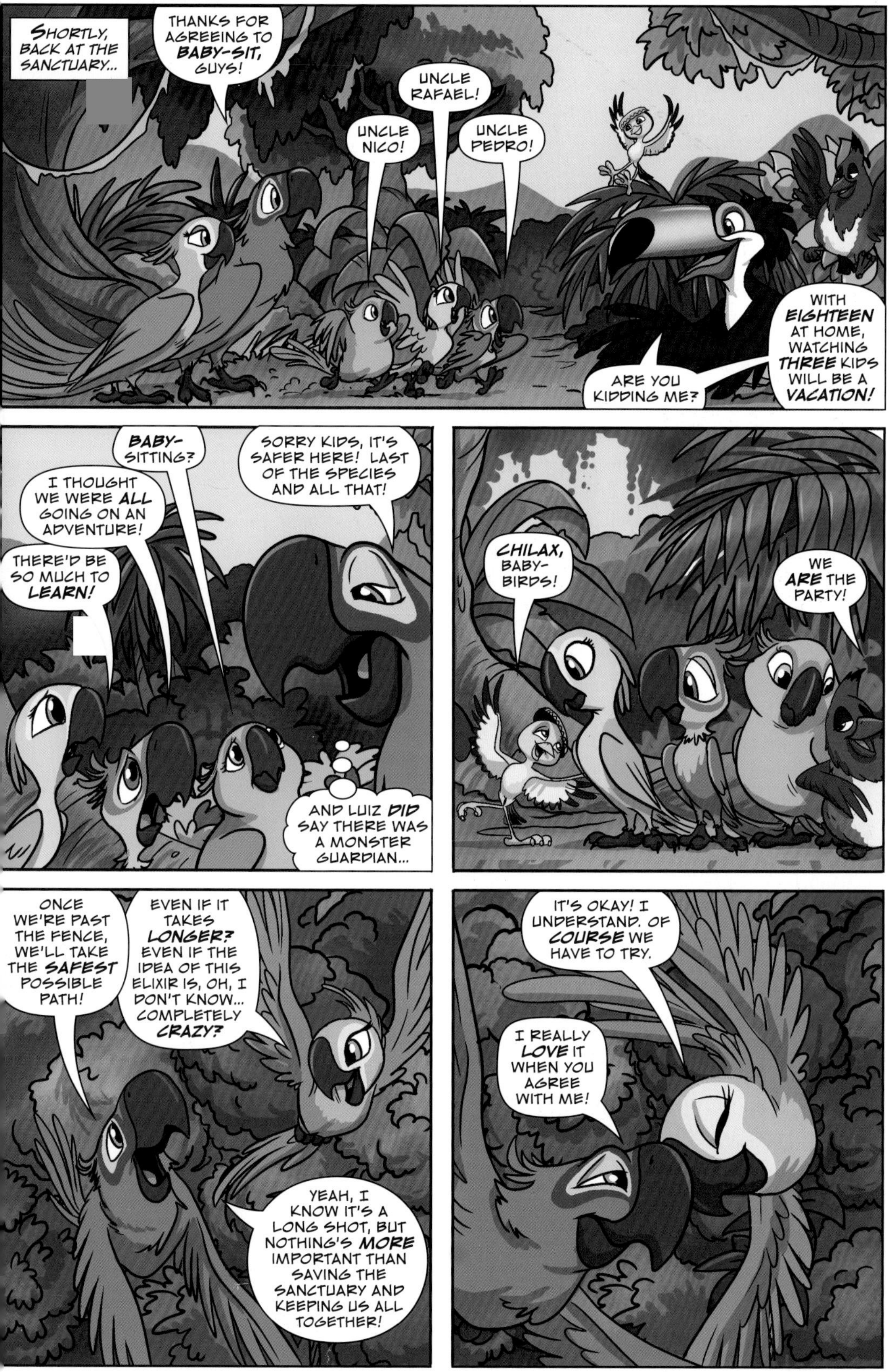
SHORTLY, BACK AT THE SANCTUARY...
THANKS FOR AGREEING TO BABY-SIT, GUYS!
UNCLE RAFAEL!
UNCLE NICO!
UNCLE PEDRO!
ARE YOU KIDDING ME?
WITH EIGHTEEN AT HOME, WATCHING THREE KIDS WILL BE A VACATION!
BABY-SITTING?
I THOUGHT WE WERE ALL GOING ON AN ADVENTURE!
THERE'D BE SO MUCH TO LEARN!
SORRY KIDS, IT'S SAFER HERE! LAST OF THE SPECIES AND ALL THAT!
AND LUIZ DID SAY THERE WAS A MONSTER GUARDIAN...
CHILAX, BABY-BIRDS!
WE ARE THE PARTY!
ONCE WE'RE PAST THE FENCE, WE'LL TAKE THE SAFEST POSSIBLE PATH!
EVEN IF IT TAKES LONGER? EVEN IF THE IDEA OF THIS ELIXIR IS, OH, I DON'T KNOW... COMPLETELY CRAZY?
YEAH, I KNOW IT'S A LONG SHOT, BUT NOTHING'S MORE IMPORTANT THAN SAVING THE SANCTUARY AND KEEPING US ALL TOGETHER!
IT'S OKAY! I UNDERSTAND. OF COURSE WE HAVE TO TRY.
I REALLY LOVE IT WHEN YOU AGREE WITH ME!

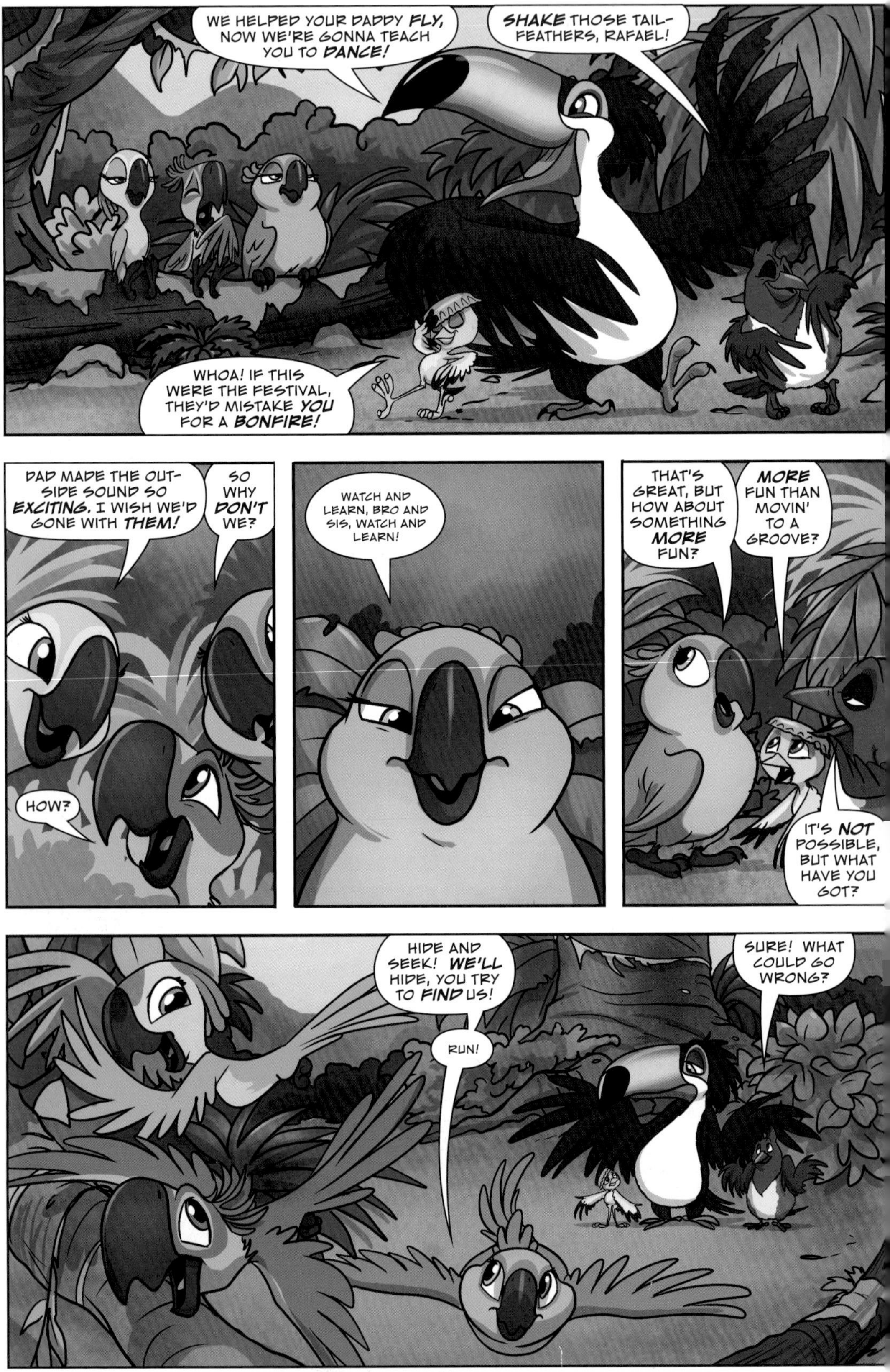
WE HELPED YOUR DADDY FLY, NOW WE'RE GONNA TEACH YOU TO DANCE!
SHAKE THOSE TAIL-FEATHERS, RAFAEL!
WHOA! IF THIS WERE THE FESTIVAL, THEY'D MISTAKE YOU FOR A BONFIRE!
DAD MADE THE OUTSIDE SOUND SO EXCITING. I WISH WE'D GONE WITH THEM!
SO WHY DON'T WE?
HOW?
WATCH AND LEARN, BRO AND SIS, WATCH AND LEARN!
THAT'S GREAT, BUT HOW ABOUT SOMETHING MORE FUN?
MORE FUN THAN MOVIN' TO A GROOVE?
IT'S NOT POSSIBLE, BUT WHAT HAVE YOU GOT?
HIDE AND SEEK! WE'LL HIDE, YOU TRY TO FIND US!
RUN!
SURE! WHAT COULD GO WRONG?

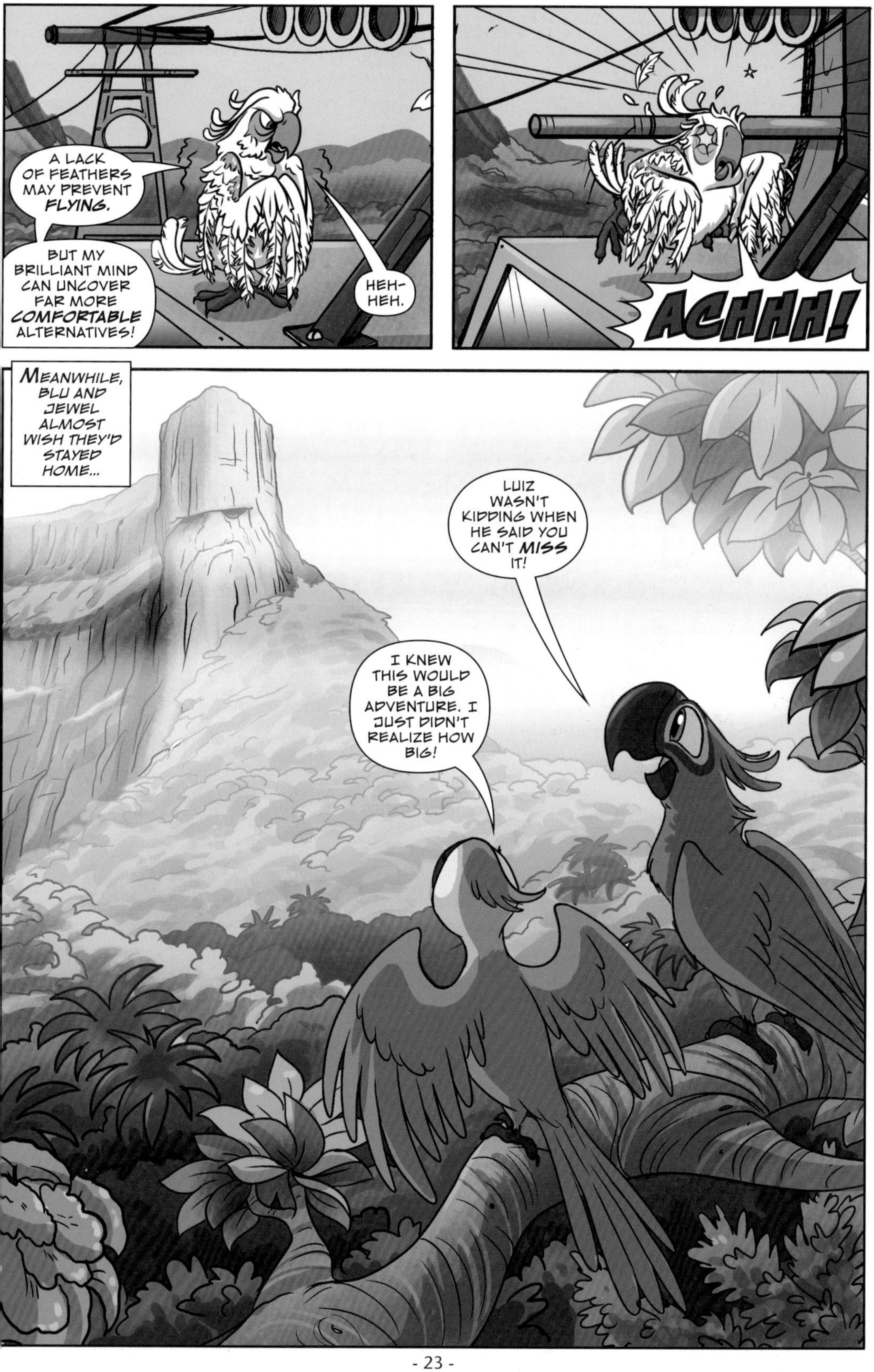
A LACK OF FEATHERS MAY PREVENT FLYING.
BUT MY BRILLIANT MIND CAN UNCOVER FAR MORE COMFORTABLE ALTERNATIVES!
HEH-HEH.
ACHHH!
MEANWHILE, BLU AND JEWEL ALMOST WISH THEY'D STAYED HOME...
LUIZ WASN'T KIDDING WHEN HE SAID YOU CAN'T MISS IT!
I KNEW THIS WOULD BE A BIG ADVENTURE. I JUST DIDN'T REALIZE HOW BIG!

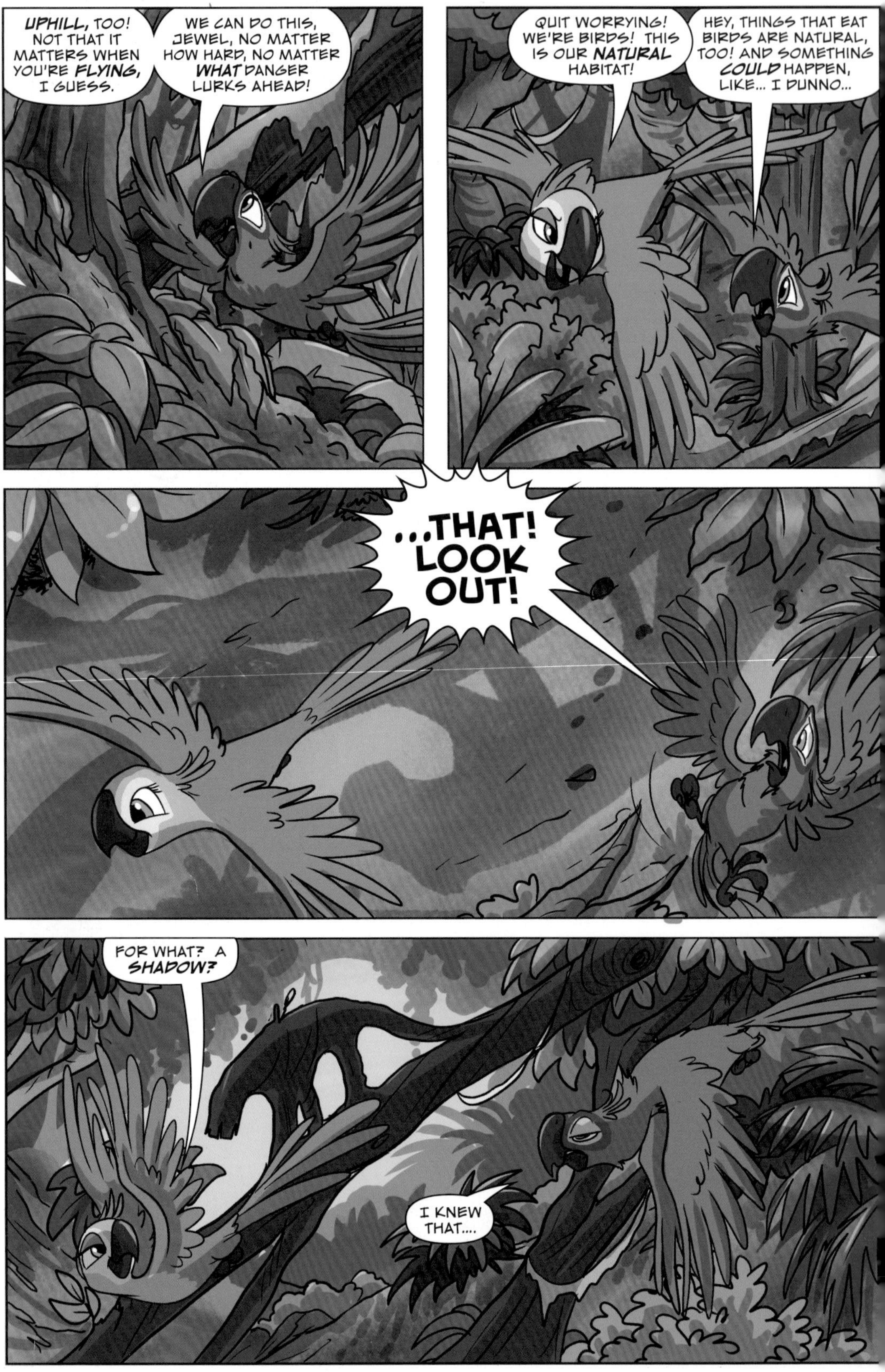
UPHILL, TOO! NOT THAT IT MATTERS WHEN YOU'RE FLYING, I GUESS.
WE CAN DO THIS, JEWEL, NO MATTER HOW HARD, NO MATTER WHAT DANGER LURKS AHEAD!
QUIT WORRYING! WE'RE BIRDS! THIS IS OUR NATURAL HABITAT!
HEY, THINGS THAT EAT BIRDS ARE NATURAL, TOO! AND SOMETHING COULD HAPPEN, LIKE... I DUNNO...
...THAT! LOOK OUT!
FOR WHAT? A SHADOW?
I KNEW THAT....

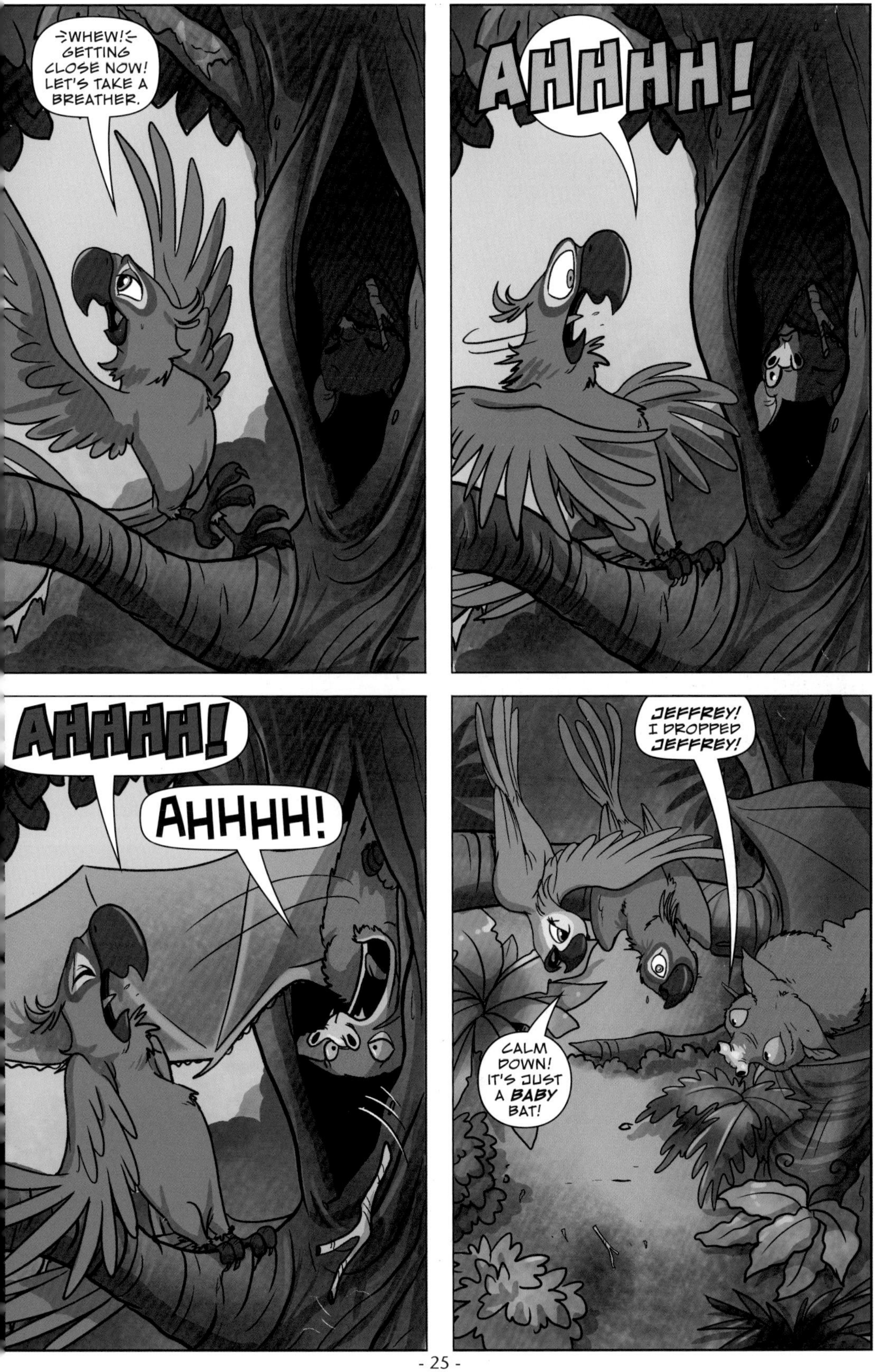

WHEW! GETTING CLOSE NOW! LET'S TAKE A BREATHER.
AHHHH!
AHHHH!
AHHHH!
JEFFREY! I DROPPED JEFFREY!
CALM DOWN! IT'S JUST A *BABY* BAT!

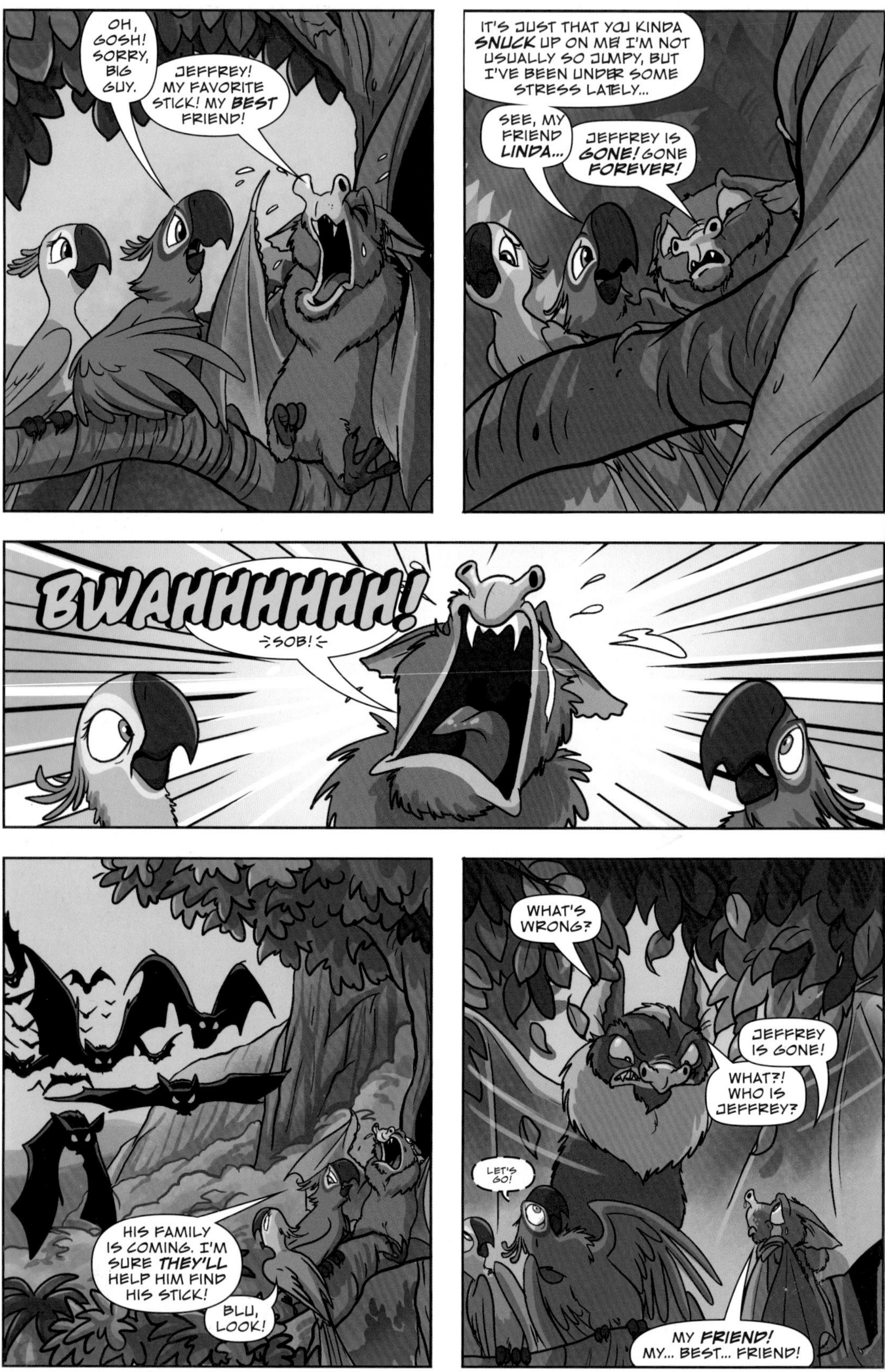
OH, GOSH! SORRY, BIG GUY.
JEFFREY! MY FAVORITE STICK! MY BEST FRIEND!
IT'S JUST THAT YOU KINDA SNUCK UP ON ME! I'M NOT USUALLY SO JUMPY, BUT I'VE BEEN UNDER SOME STRESS LATELY...
SEE, MY FRIEND LINDA...
JEFFREY IS GONE! GONE FOREVER!
BWAHHHHHHH!
SOB!
HIS FAMILY IS COMING. I'M SURE THEY'LL HELP HIM FIND HIS STICK!
BLU, LOOK!
WHAT'S WRONG?
JEFFREY IS GONE!
WHAT?! WHO IS JEFFREY?
LET'S GO!
MY FRIEND! MY... BEST... FRIEND!

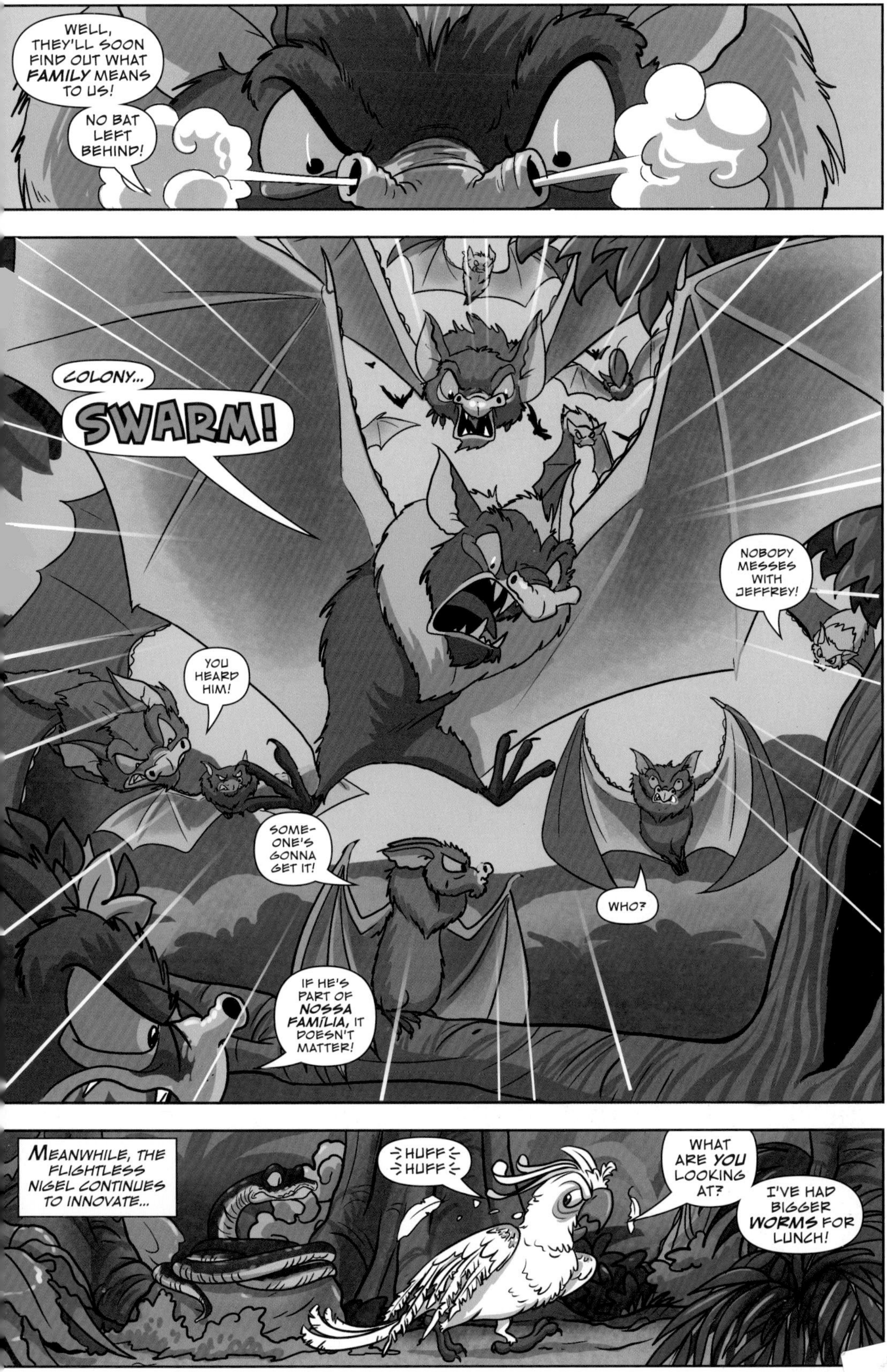
WELL, THEY'LL SOON FIND OUT WHAT FAMILY MEANS TO US!
NO BAT LEFT BEHIND!
COLONY...
SWARM!
NOBODY MESSES WITH JEFFREY!
YOU HEARD HIM!
SOME-ONE'S GONNA GET IT!
WHO?
IF HE'S PART OF NOSSA FAMÍLIA, IT DOESN'T MATTER!
MEANWHILE, THE FLIGHTLESS NIGEL CONTINUES TO INNOVATE...
HUFF HUFF
WHAT ARE YOU LOOKING AT?
I'VE HAD BIGGER WORMS FOR LUNCH!

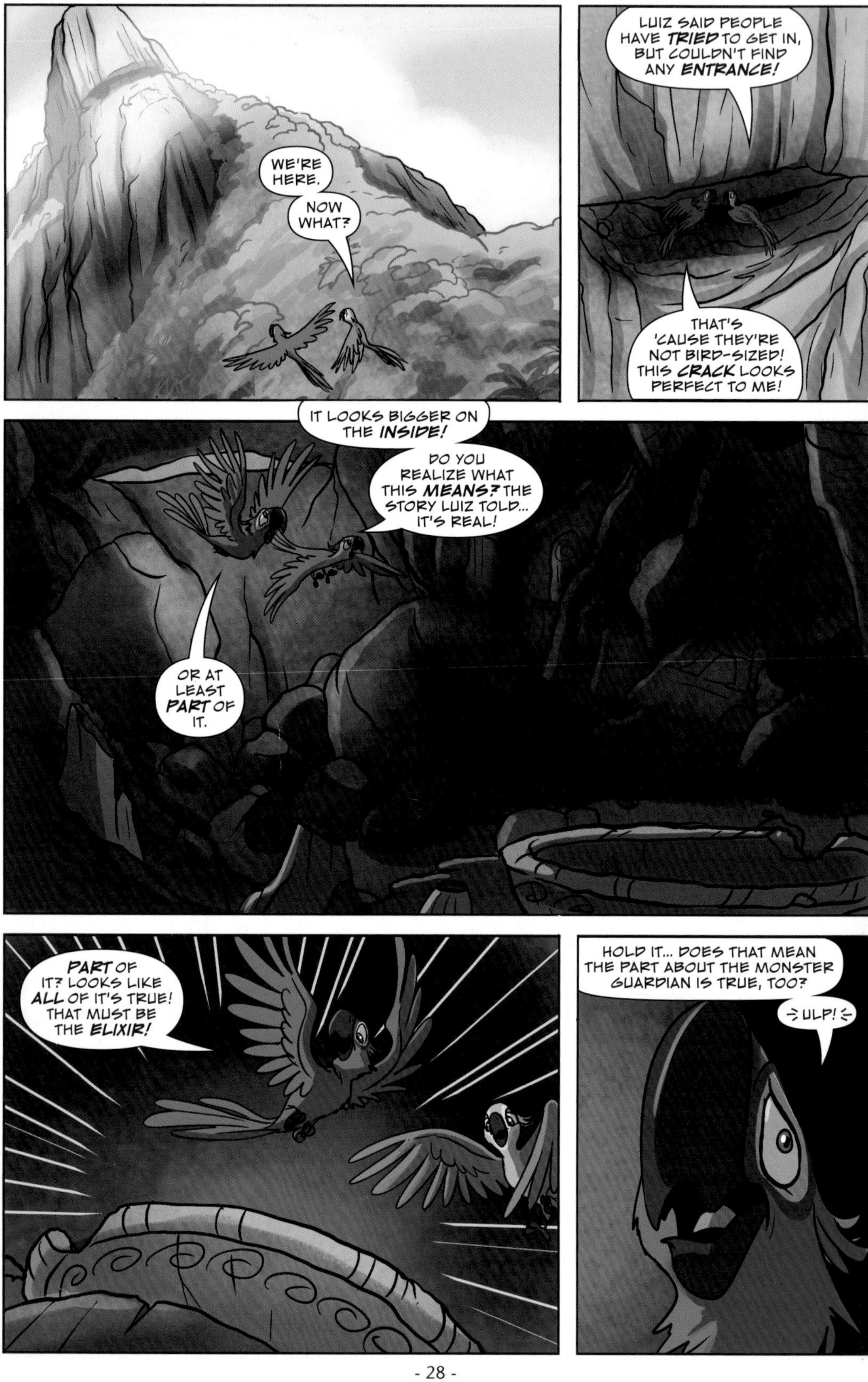
WE'RE HERE.
NOW WHAT?
LUIZ SAID PEOPLE HAVE TRIED TO GET IN, BUT COULDN'T FIND ANY ENTRANCE!
THAT'S 'CAUSE THEY'RE NOT BIRD-SIZED! THIS CRACK LOOKS PERFECT TO ME!
IT LOOKS BIGGER ON THE INSIDE!
DO YOU REALIZE WHAT THIS MEANS? THE STORY LUIZ TOLD... IT'S REAL!
OR AT LEAST PART OF IT.
PART OF IT? LOOKS LIKE ALL OF IT'S TRUE! THAT MUST BE THE ELIXIR!
HOLD IT... DOES THAT MEAN THE PART ABOUT THE MONSTER GUARDIAN IS TRUE, TOO?
ULP!

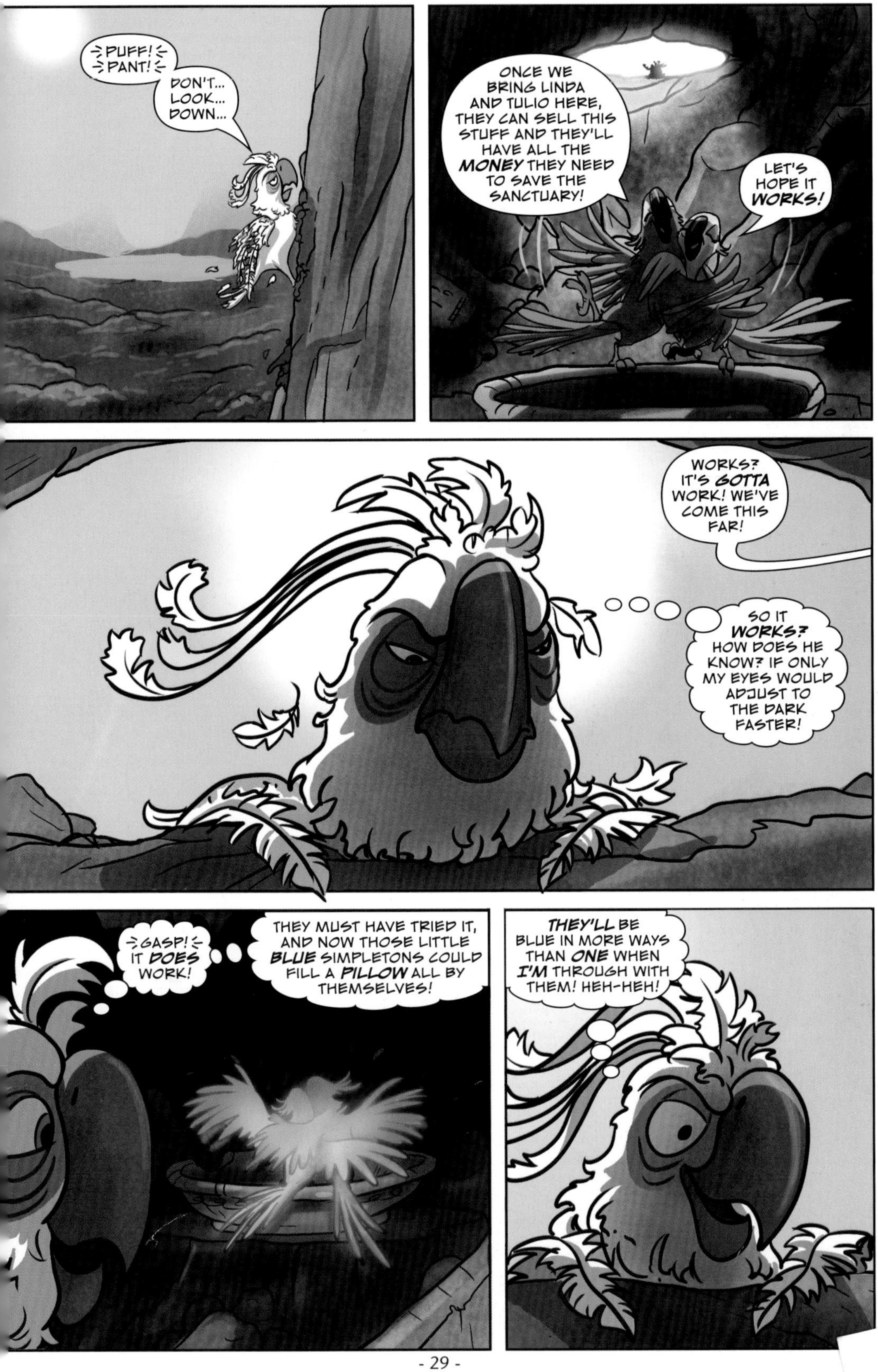
PUFF! PANT!
DON'T... LOOK... DOWN...
ONCE WE BRING LINDA AND TULIO HERE, THEY CAN SELL THIS STUFF AND THEY'LL HAVE ALL THE MONEY THEY NEED TO SAVE THE SANCTUARY!
LET'S HOPE IT WORKS!
WORKS? IT'S GOTTA WORK! WE'VE COME THIS FAR!
SO IT WORKS? HOW DOES HE KNOW? IF ONLY MY EYES WOULD ADJUST TO THE DARK FASTER!
GASP! IT DOES WORK!
THEY MUST HAVE TRIED IT, AND NOW THOSE LITTLE BLUE SIMPLETONS COULD FILL A PILLOW ALL BY THEMSELVES!
THEY'LL BE BLUE IN MORE WAYS THAN ONE WHEN I'M THROUGH WITH THEM! HEH-HEH!

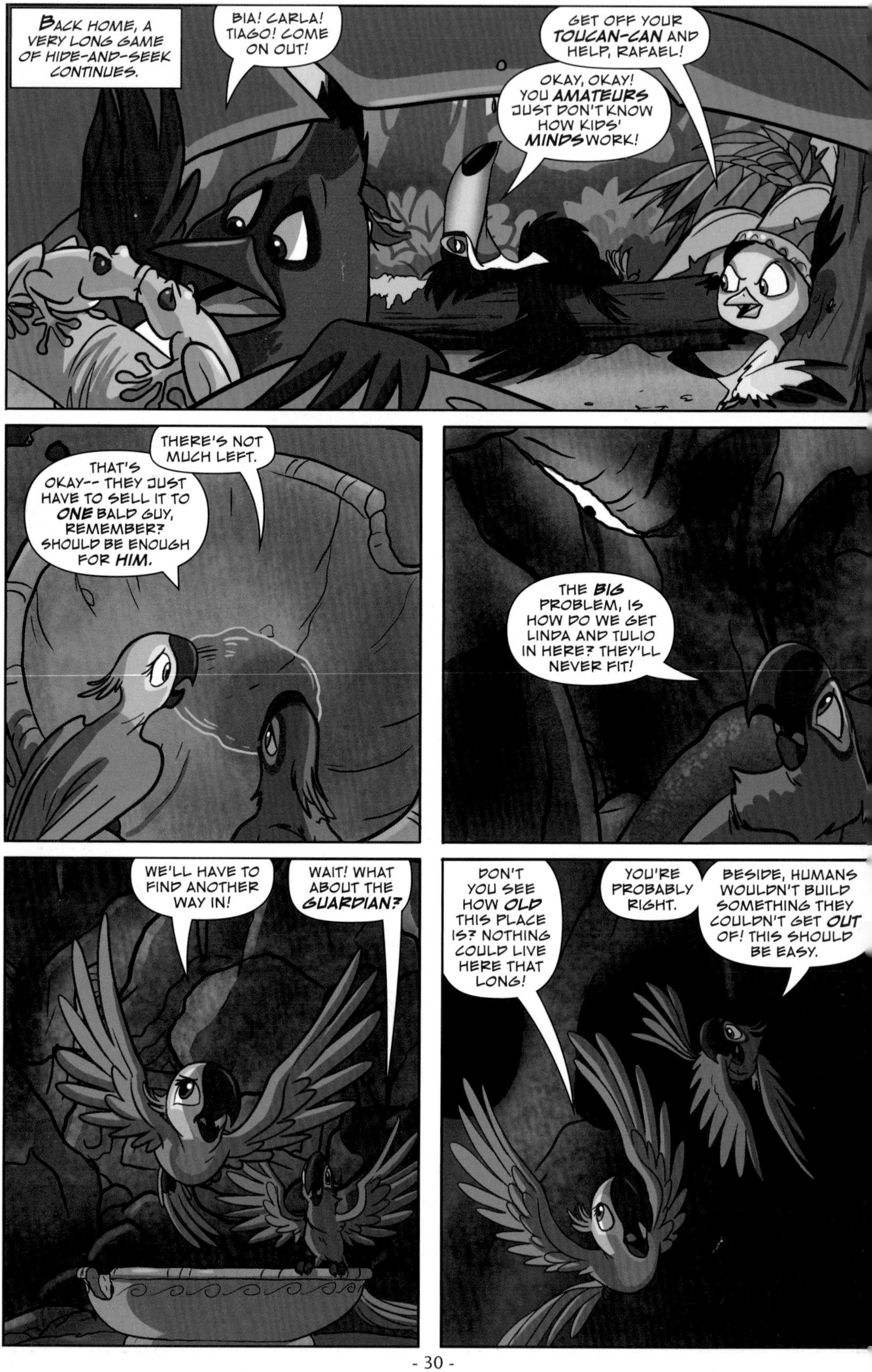
BACK HOME, A VERY LONG GAME OF HIDE-AND-SEEK CONTINUES.
BIA! CARLA! TIAGO! COME ON OUT!
GET OFF YOUR TOUCAN-CAN AND HELP, RAFAEL!
OKAY, OKAY! YOU AMATEURS JUST DON'T KNOW HOW KIDS' MINDS WORK!
THERE'S NOT MUCH LEFT.
THAT'S OKAY-- THEY JUST HAVE TO SELL IT TO ONE BALD GUY, REMEMBER? SHOULD BE ENOUGH FOR HIM.
THE BIG PROBLEM, IS HOW DO WE GET LINDA AND TULIO IN HERE? THEY'LL NEVER FIT!
WE'LL HAVE TO FIND ANOTHER WAY IN!
WAIT! WHAT ABOUT THE GUARDIAN?
DON'T YOU SEE HOW OLD THIS PLACE IS? NOTHING COULD LIVE HERE THAT LONG!
YOU'RE PROBABLY RIGHT.
BESIDE, HUMANS WOULDN'T BUILD SOMETHING THEY COULDN'T GET OUT OF! THIS SHOULD BE EASY.

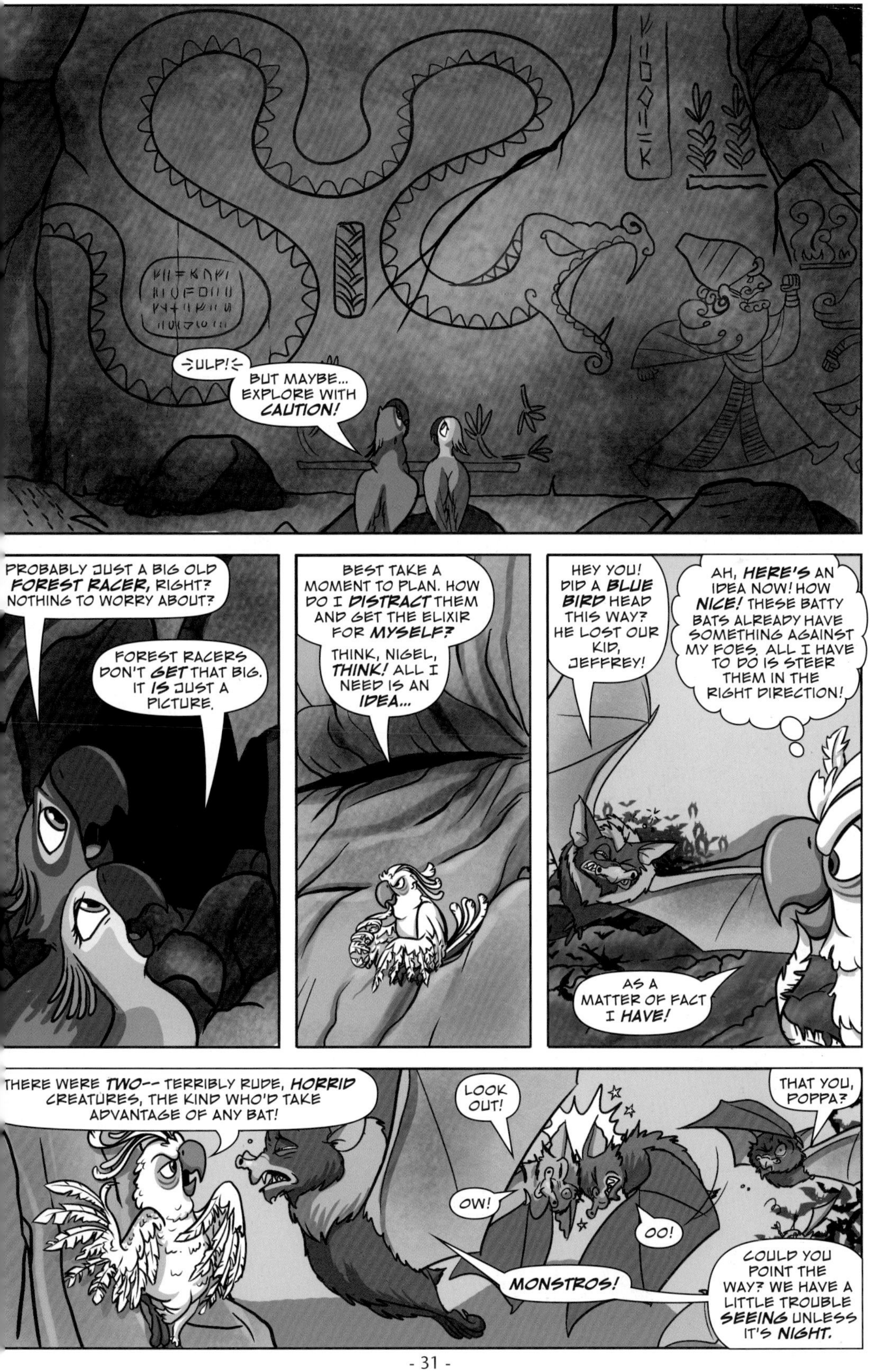
ULP!
BUT MAYBE... EXPLORE WITH CAUTION!
PROBABLY JUST A BIG OLD FOREST RACER, RIGHT? NOTHING TO WORRY ABOUT?
FOREST RACERS DON'T GET THAT BIG. IT IS JUST A PICTURE.
BEST TAKE A MOMENT TO PLAN. HOW DO I DISTRACT THEM AND GET THE ELIXIR FOR MYSELF?
THINK, NIGEL, THINK! ALL I NEED IS AN IDEA...
HEY YOU! DID A BLUE BIRD HEAD THIS WAY? HE LOST OUR KID, JEFFREY!
AH, HERE'S AN IDEA NOW! HOW NICE! THESE BATTY BATS ALREADY HAVE SOMETHING AGAINST MY FOES. ALL I HAVE TO DO IS STEER THEM IN THE RIGHT DIRECTION!
AS A MATTER OF FACT I HAVE!
THERE WERE TWO-- TERRIBLY RUDE, HORRID CREATURES, THE KIND WHO'D TAKE ADVANTAGE OF ANY BAT!
LOOK OUT!
OW!
OO!
THAT YOU, POPPA?
MONSTROS!
COULD YOU POINT THE WAY? WE HAVE A LITTLE TROUBLE SEEING UNLESS IT'S NIGHT.

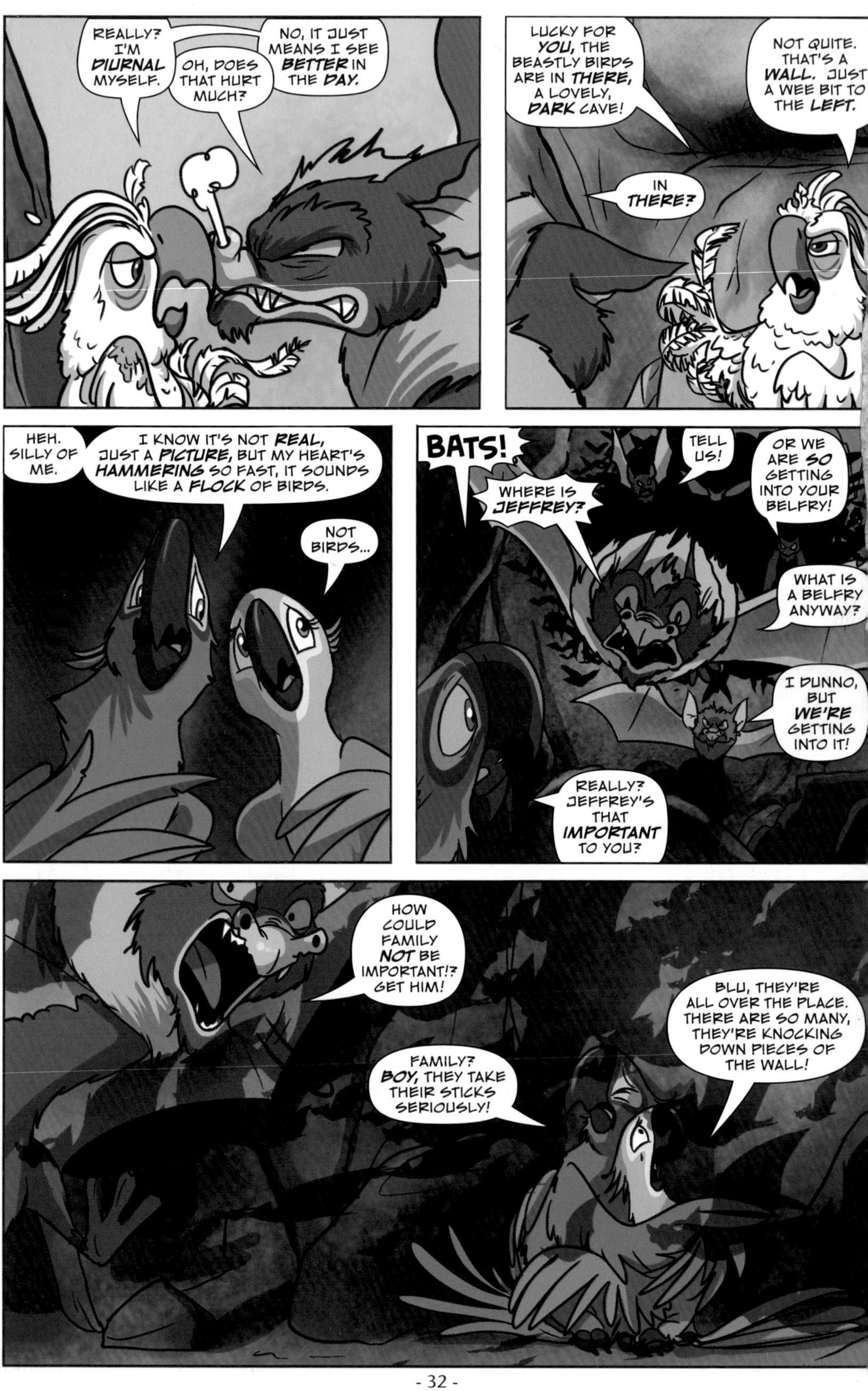
REALLY? I'M DIURNAL MYSELF.
OH, DOES THAT HURT MUCH?
NO, IT JUST MEANS I SEE BETTER IN THE DAY.
LUCKY FOR YOU, THE BEASTLY BIRDS ARE IN THERE, A LOVELY, DARK CAVE!
IN THERE?
NOT QUITE. THAT'S A WALL. JUST A WEE BIT TO THE LEFT.
HEH. SILLY OF ME.
I KNOW IT'S NOT REAL, JUST A PICTURE, BUT MY HEART'S HAMMERING SO FAST, IT SOUNDS LIKE A FLOCK OF BIRDS.
NOT BIRDS...
BATS!
WHERE IS JEFFREY?
TELL US!
OR WE ARE SO GETTING INTO YOUR BELFRY!
WHAT IS A BELFRY ANYWAY?
I DUNNO, BUT WE'RE GETTING INTO IT!
REALLY? JEFFREY'S THAT IMPORTANT TO YOU?
HOW COULD FAMILY NOT BE IMPORTANT!? GET HIM!
FAMILY? BOY, THEY TAKE THEIR STICKS SERIOUSLY!
BLU, THEY'RE ALL OVER THE PLACE. THERE ARE SO MANY, THEY'RE KNOCKING DOWN PIECES OF THE WALL!

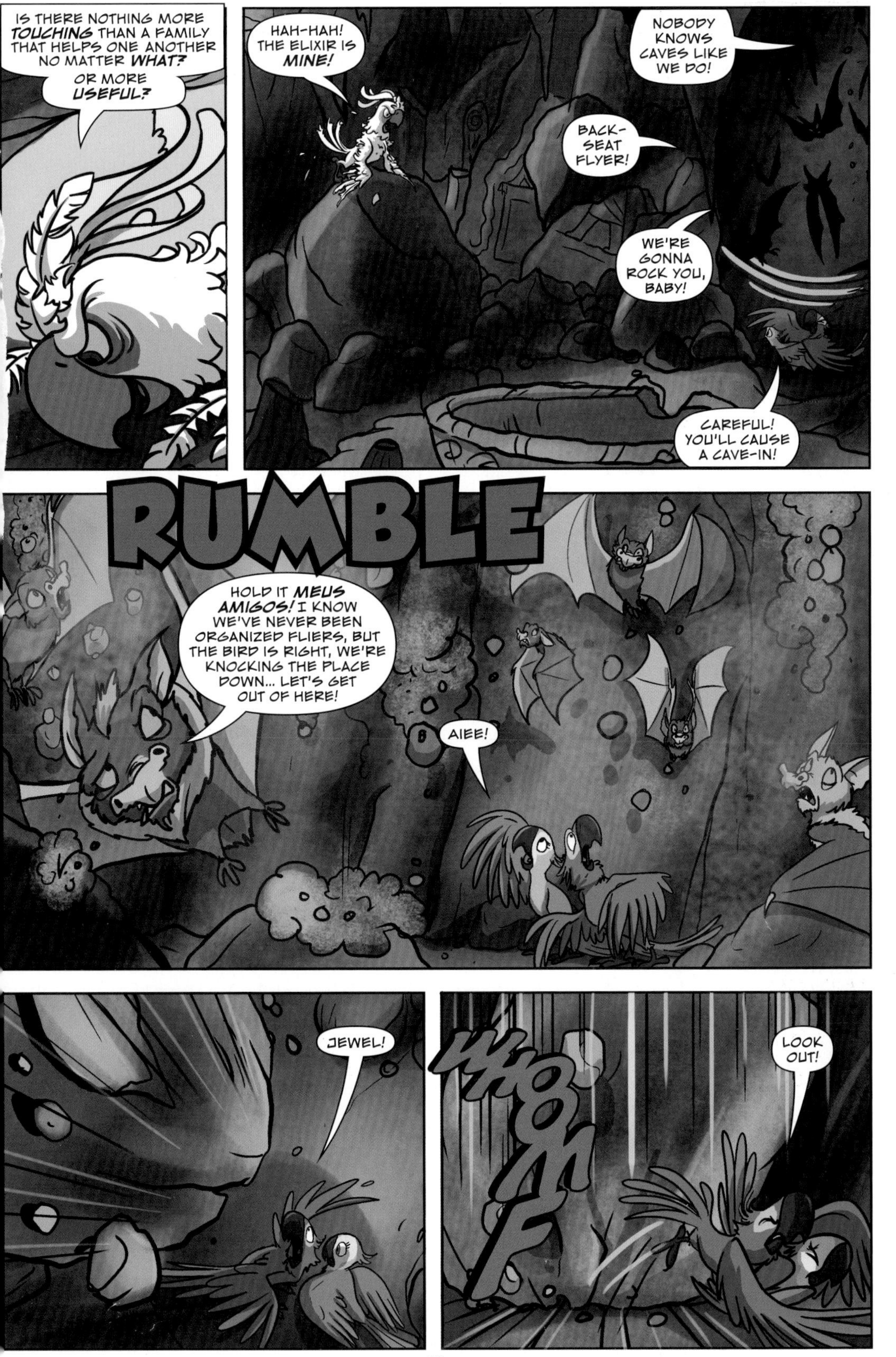
IS THERE NOTHING MORE *TOUCHING* THAN A FAMILY THAT HELPS ONE ANOTHER NO MATTER *WHAT?*
OR MORE *USEFUL?*
HAH-HAH! THE ELIXIR IS *MINE!*
NOBODY KNOWS CAVES LIKE WE DO!
BACK-SEAT FLYER!
WE'RE GONNA ROCK YOU, BABY!
CAREFUL! YOU'LL CAUSE A CAVE-IN!
RUMBLE
HOLD IT *MEUS AMIGOS!* I KNOW WE'VE NEVER BEEN ORGANIZED FLIERS, BUT THE BIRD IS RIGHT, WE'RE KNOCKING THE PLACE DOWN... LET'S GET OUT OF HERE!
AIEE!
JEWEL!
WHOMF
LOOK OUT!

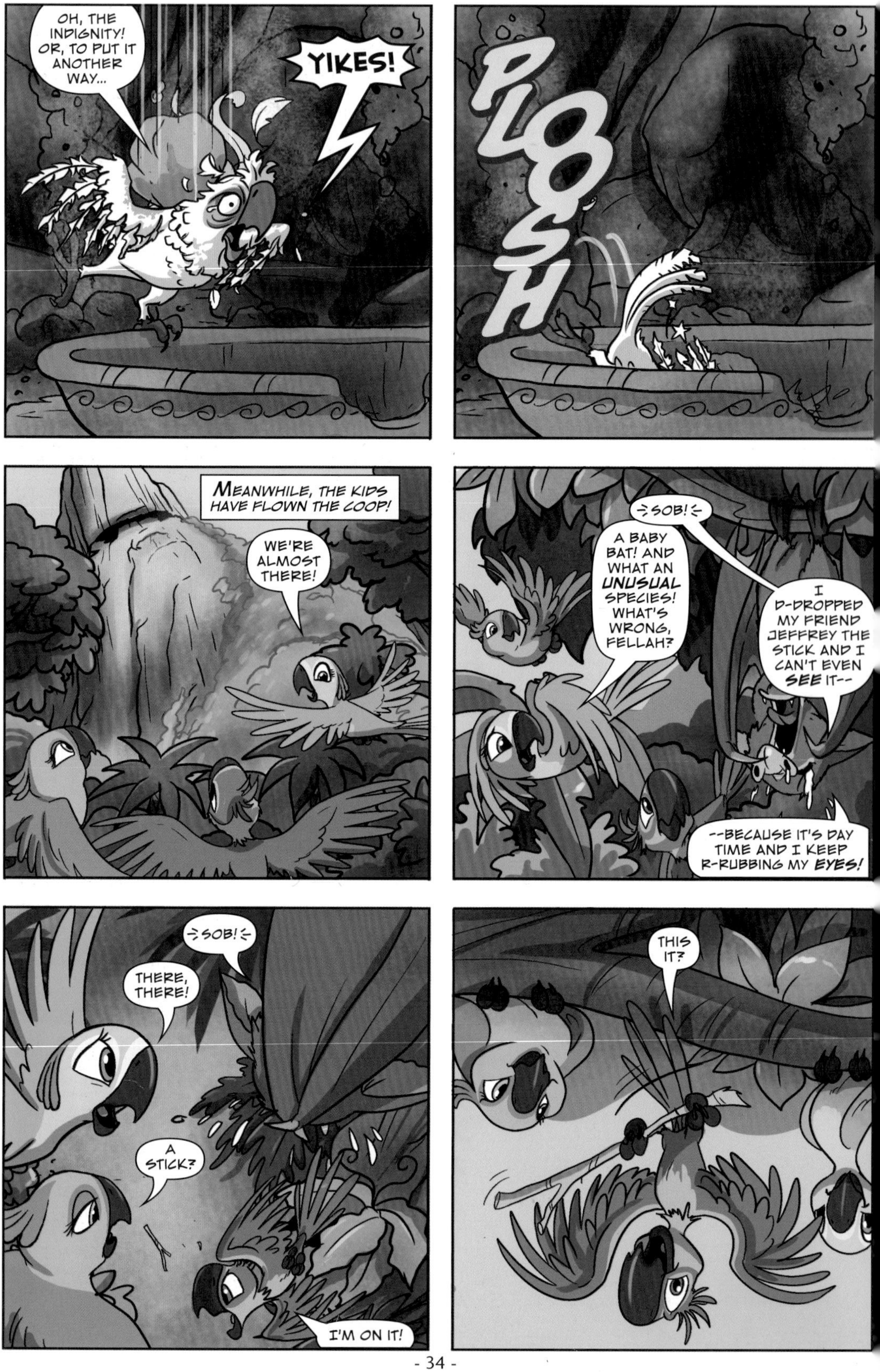
OH, THE INDIGNITY! OR, TO PUT IT ANOTHER WAY...
YIKES!
PLOOSH
MEANWHILE, THE KIDS HAVE FLOWN THE COOP!
WE'RE ALMOST THERE!
SOB!
A BABY BAT! AND WHAT AN UNUSUAL SPECIES! WHAT'S WRONG, FELLAH?
I D-DROPPED MY FRIEND JEFFREY THE STICK AND I CAN'T EVEN SEE IT--
--BECAUSE IT'S DAY TIME AND I KEEP R-RUBBING MY EYES!
SOB!
THERE, THERE!
A STICK?
I'M ON IT!
THIS IT?

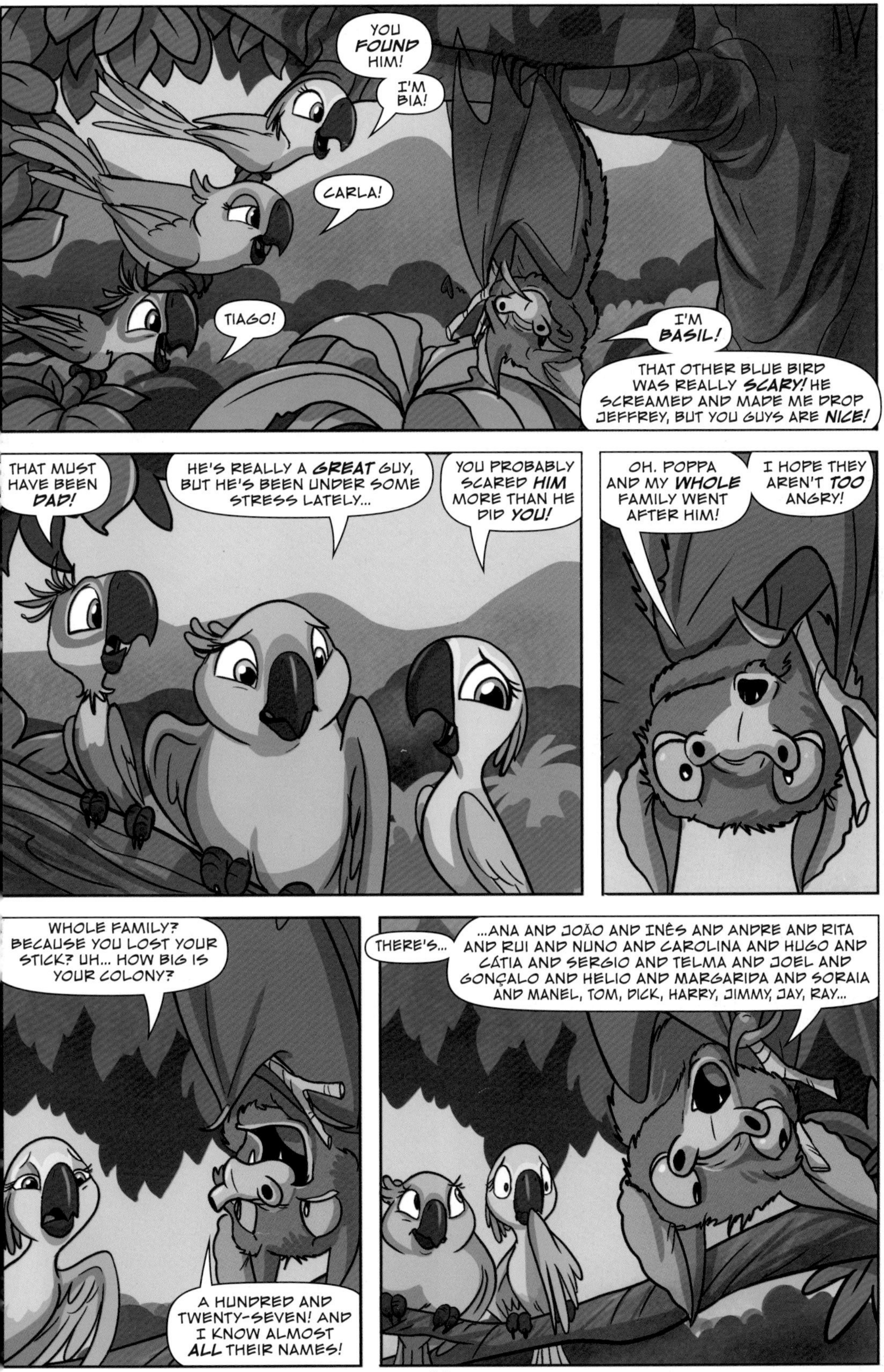
YOU FOUND HIM!
I'M BIA!
CARLA!
TIAGO!
I'M BASIL!
THAT OTHER BLUE BIRD WAS REALLY SCARY! HE SCREAMED AND MADE ME DROP JEFFREY, BUT YOU GUYS ARE NICE!
THAT MUST HAVE BEEN DAD!
HE'S REALLY A GREAT GUY, BUT HE'S BEEN UNDER SOME STRESS LATELY...
YOU PROBABLY SCARED HIM MORE THAN HE DID YOU!
OH. POPPA AND MY WHOLE FAMILY WENT AFTER HIM!
I HOPE THEY AREN'T TOO ANGRY!
WHOLE FAMILY? BECAUSE YOU LOST YOUR STICK? UH... HOW BIG IS YOUR COLONY?
A HUNDRED AND TWENTY-SEVEN! AND I KNOW ALMOST ALL THEIR NAMES!
THERE'S...
...ANA AND JOÃO AND INÊS AND ANDRE AND RITA AND RUI AND NUNO AND CAROLINA AND HUGO AND CÁTIA AND SERGIO AND TELMA AND JOEL AND GONÇALO AND HELIO AND MARGARIDA AND SORAIA AND MANEL, TOM, DICK, HARRY, JIMMY, JAY, RAY...

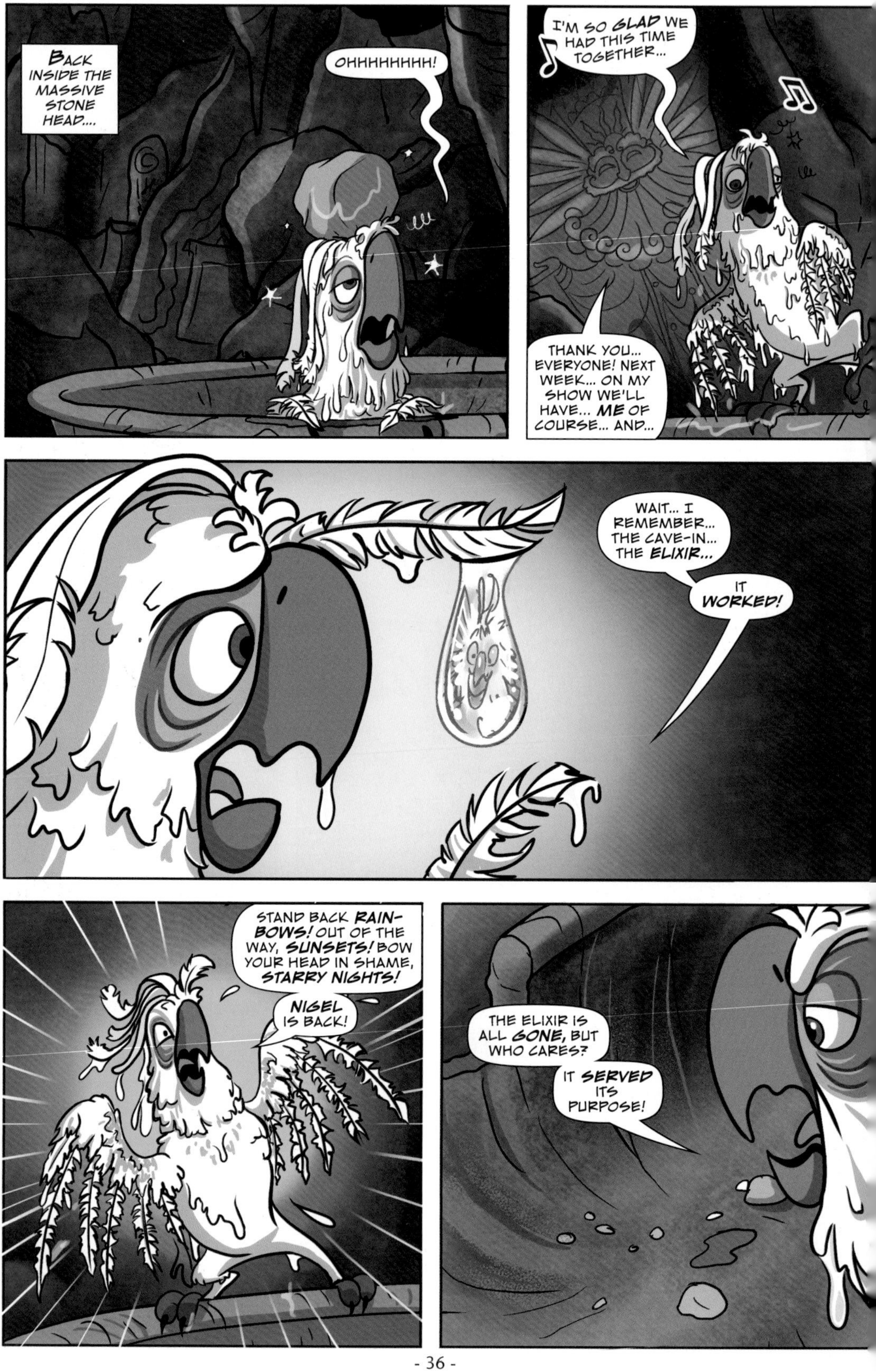
BACK INSIDE THE MASSIVE STONE HEAD....
OHHHHHHHH!
I'M SO GLAD WE HAD THIS TIME TOGETHER...
THANK YOU... EVERYONE! NEXT WEEK... ON MY SHOW WE'LL HAVE... ME OF COURSE... AND...
WAIT... I REMEMBER... THE CAVE-IN... THE ELIXIR...
IT WORKED!
STAND BACK RAIN-BOWS! OUT OF THE WAY, SUNSETS! BOW YOUR HEAD IN SHAME, STARRY NIGHTS!
NIGEL IS BACK!
THE ELIXIR IS ALL GONE, BUT WHO CARES?
IT SERVED ITS PURPOSE!

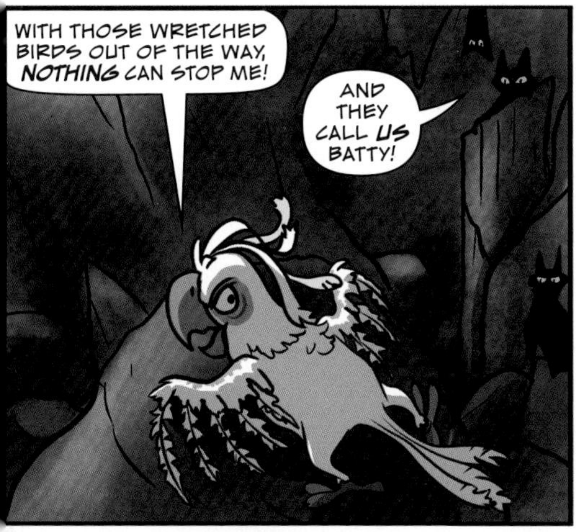
WITH THOSE WRETCHED BIRDS OUT OF THE WAY, NOTHING CAN STOP ME!
AND THEY CALL US BATTY!
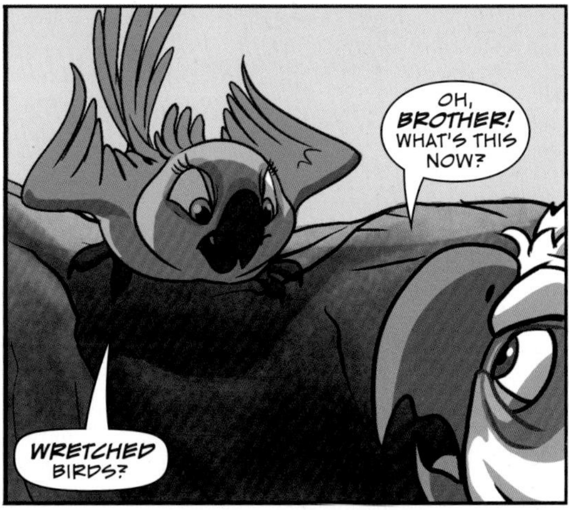
OH, BROTHER! WHAT'S THIS NOW?
WRETCHED BIRDS?
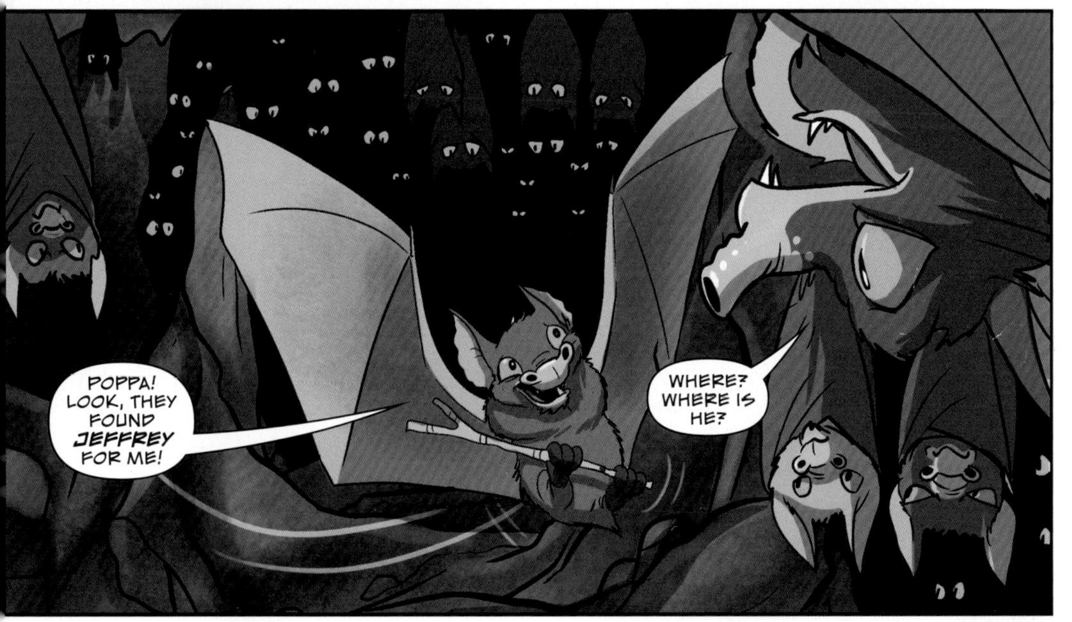
POPPA! LOOK, THEY FOUND JEFFREY FOR ME!
WHERE? WHERE IS HE?
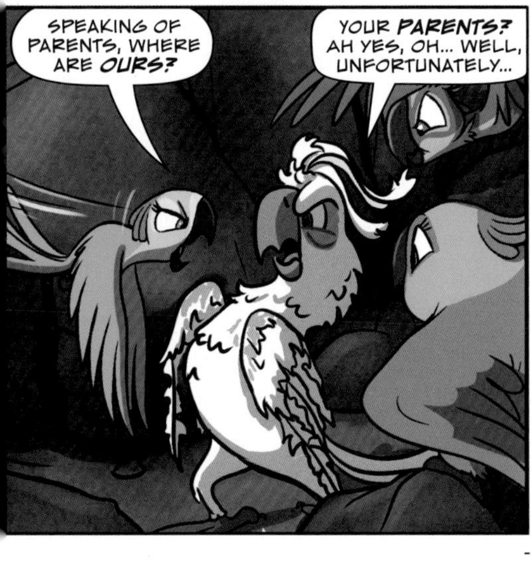
SPEAKING OF PARENTS, WHERE ARE OURS?
YOUR PARENTS? AH YES, OH... WELL, UNFORTUNATELY...
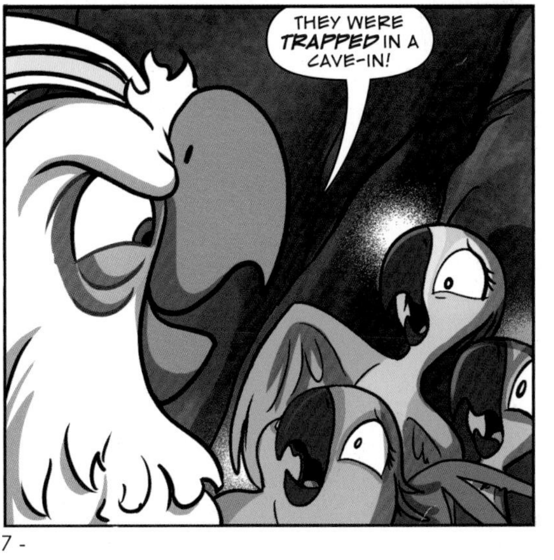
THEY WERE TRAPPED IN A CAVE-IN!

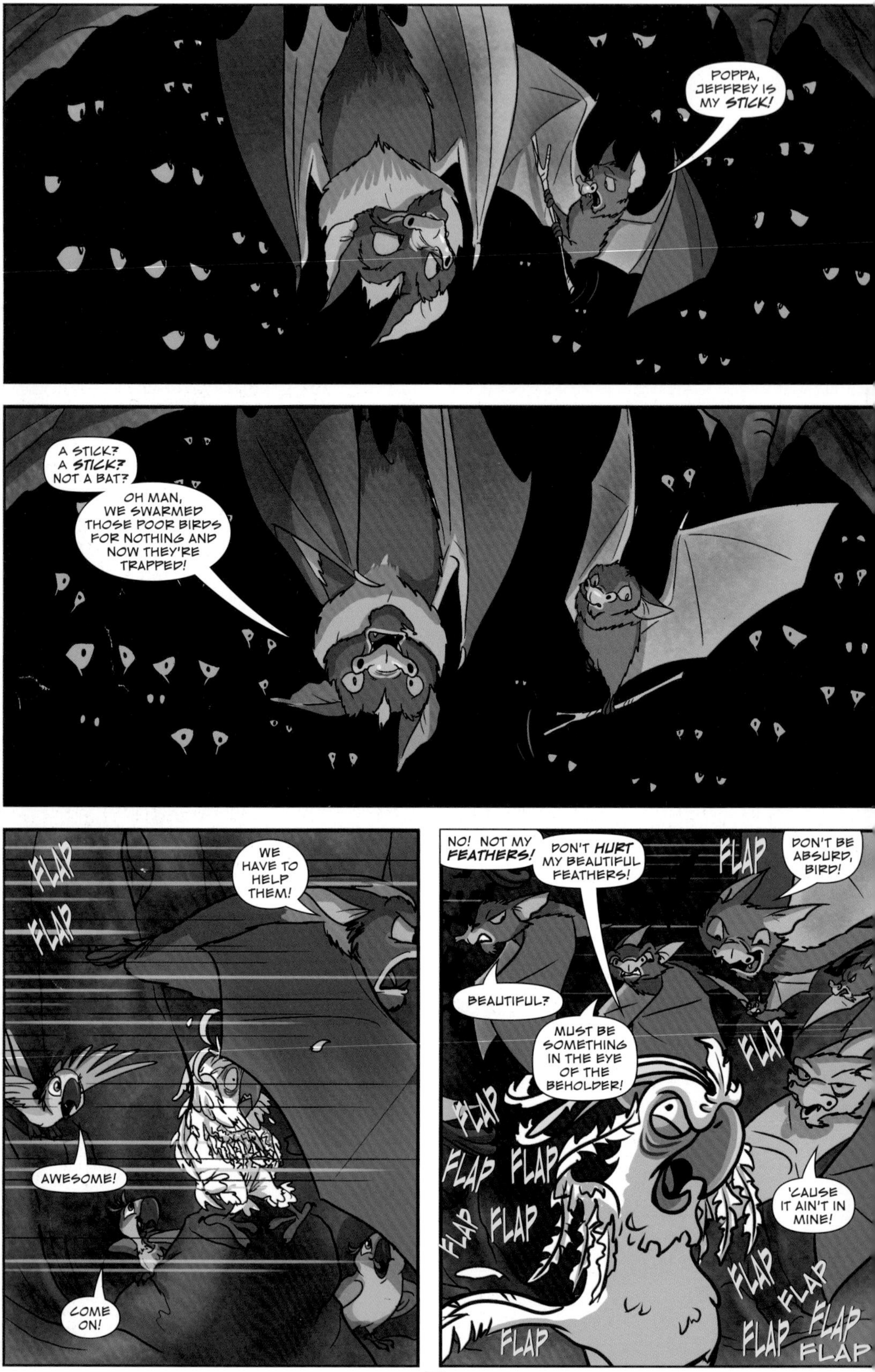
POPPA, JEFFREY IS MY STICK!
A STICK? A STICK? NOT A BAT?
OH MAN, WE SWARMED THOSE POOR BIRDS FOR NOTHING AND NOW THEY'RE TRAPPED!
FLAP
FLAP
WE HAVE TO HELP THEM!
AWESOME!
COME ON!
NO! NOT MY FEATHERS!
DON'T HURT MY BEAUTIFUL FEATHERS!
FLAP
DON'T BE ABSURD, BIRD!
BEAUTIFUL?
MUST BE SOMETHING IN THE EYE OF THE BEHOLDER!
FLAP
FLAP FLAP FLAP
FLAP FLAP
'CAUSE IT AIN'T IN MINE!
FLAP FLAP FLAP FLAP FLAP FLAP

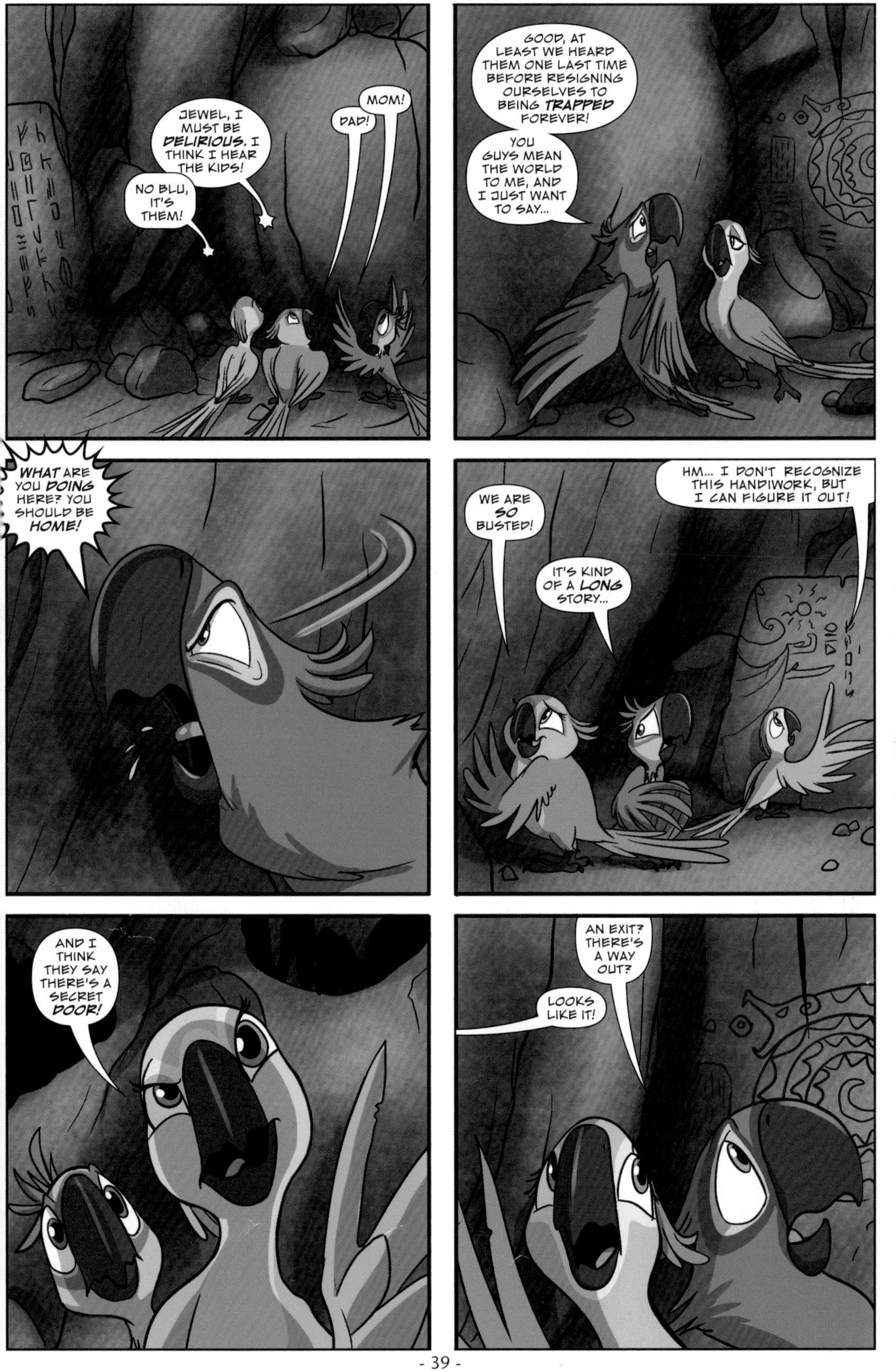
JEWEL, I MUST BE DELIRIOUS. I THINK I HEAR THE KIDS!
NO BLU, IT'S THEM!
DAD!
MOM!
GOOD, AT LEAST WE HEARD THEM ONE LAST TIME BEFORE RESIGNING OURSELVES TO BEING TRAPPED FOREVER!
YOU GUYS MEAN THE WORLD TO ME, AND I JUST WANT TO SAY...
WHAT ARE YOU DOING HERE? YOU SHOULD BE HOME!
WE ARE SO BUSTED!
IT'S KIND OF A LONG STORY...
HM... I DON'T RECOGNIZE THIS HANDIWORK, BUT I CAN FIGURE IT OUT!
AND I THINK THEY SAY THERE'S A SECRET DOOR!
AN EXIT? THERE'S A WAY OUT?
LOOKS LIKE IT!

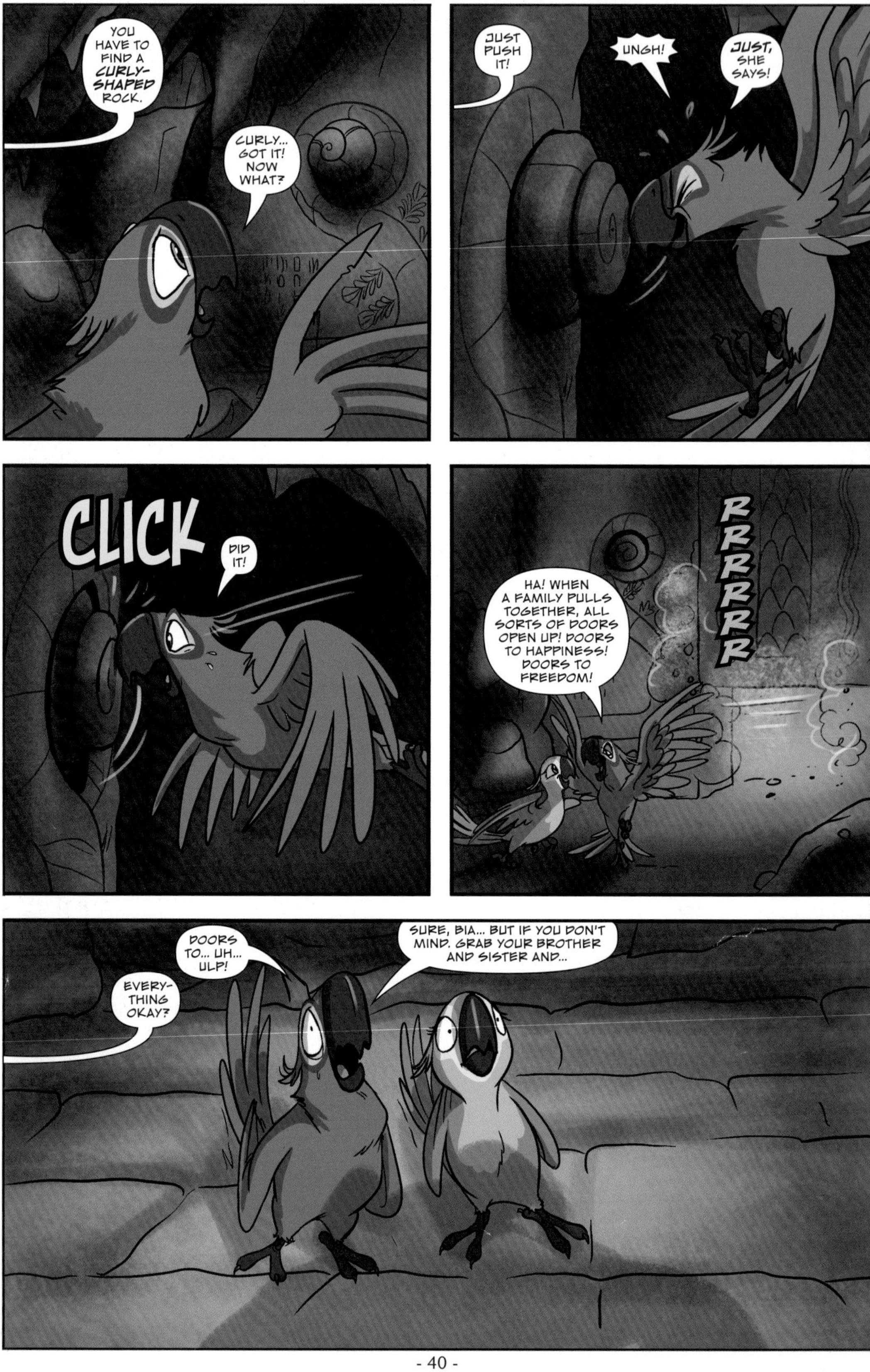
YOU HAVE TO FIND A CURLY-SHAPED ROCK.
CURLY... GOT IT! NOW WHAT?
JUST PUSH IT!
UNGH!
JUST, SHE SAYS!
CLICK
DID IT!
RRRRRR
HA! WHEN A FAMILY PULLS TOGETHER, ALL SORTS OF DOORS OPEN UP! DOORS TO HAPPINESS! DOORS TO FREEDOM!
EVERY-THING OKAY?
DOORS TO... UH... ULP!
SURE, BIA... BUT IF YOU DON'T MIND. GRAB YOUR BROTHER AND SISTER AND...

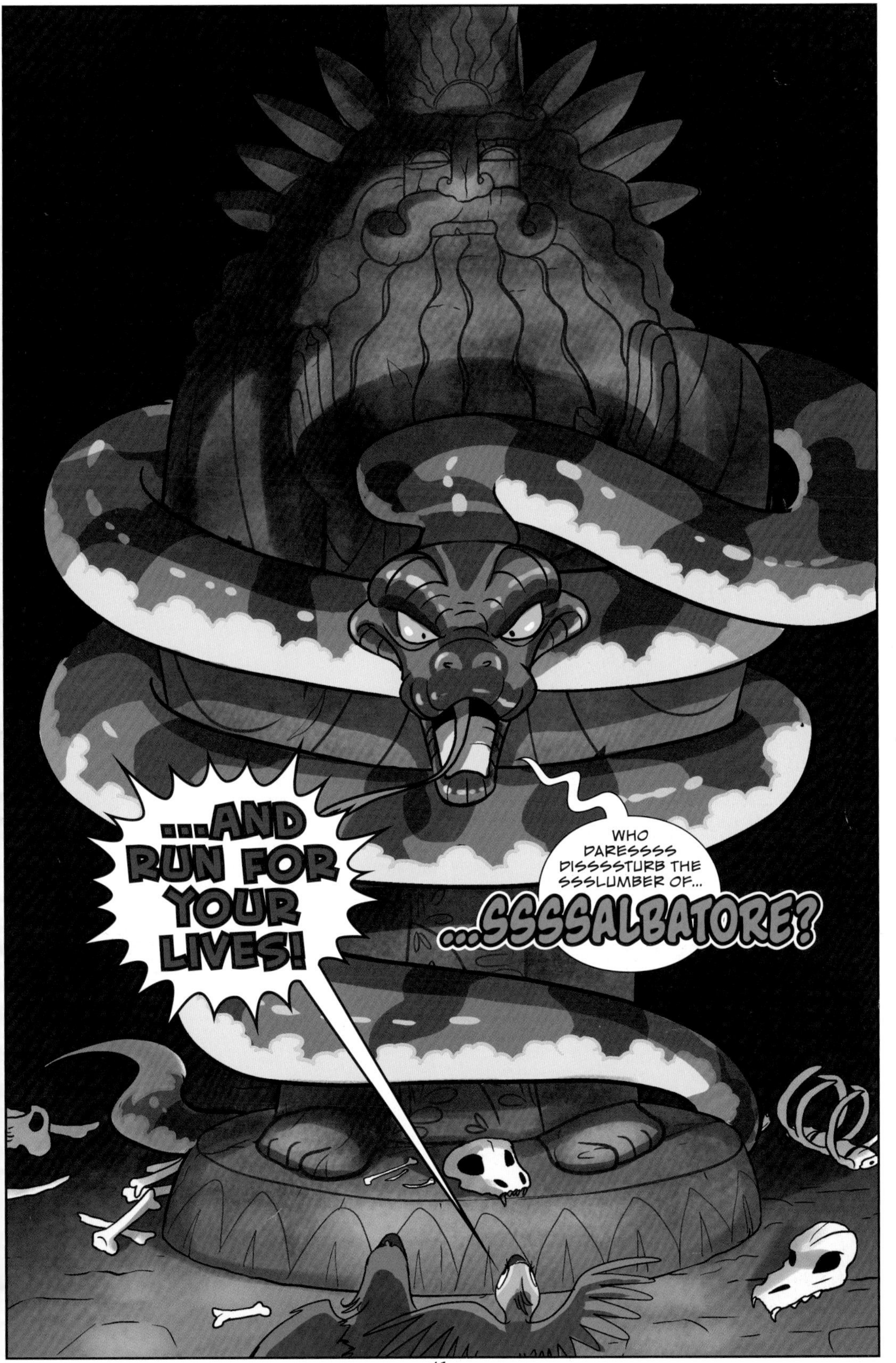
WHO DARESSSS DISSSSSTURB THE SSSLUMBER OF...
...SSSSALBATORE?
...AND RUN FOR YOUR LIVES!

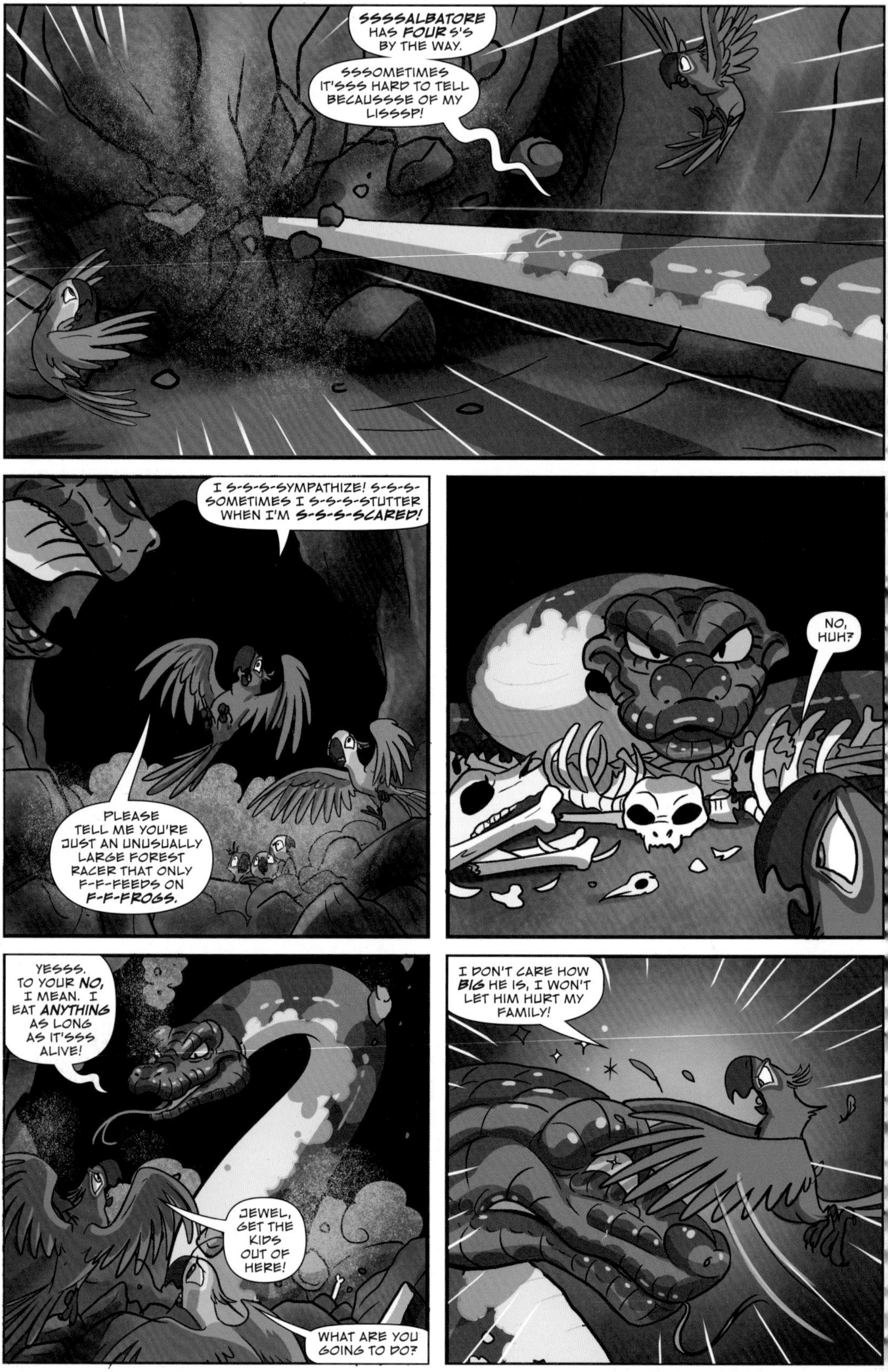
SSSSALBATORE HAS FOUR S'S BY THE WAY.
SSSOMETIMES IT'SSS HARD TO TELL BECAUSSSE OF MY LISSSP!
I S-S-S-SYMPATHIZE! S-S-S-SOMETIMES I S-S-S-STUTTER WHEN I'M S-S-S-SCARED!
PLEASE TELL ME YOU'RE JUST AN UNUSUALLY LARGE FOREST RACER THAT ONLY F-F-FEEDS ON F-F-FROGS.
NO, HUH?
YESSS. TO YOUR NO, I MEAN. I EAT ANYTHING AS LONG AS IT'SSS ALIVE!
JEWEL, GET THE KIDS OUT OF HERE!
WHAT ARE YOU GOING TO DO?
I DON'T CARE HOW BIG HE IS, I WON'T LET HIM HURT MY FAMILY!

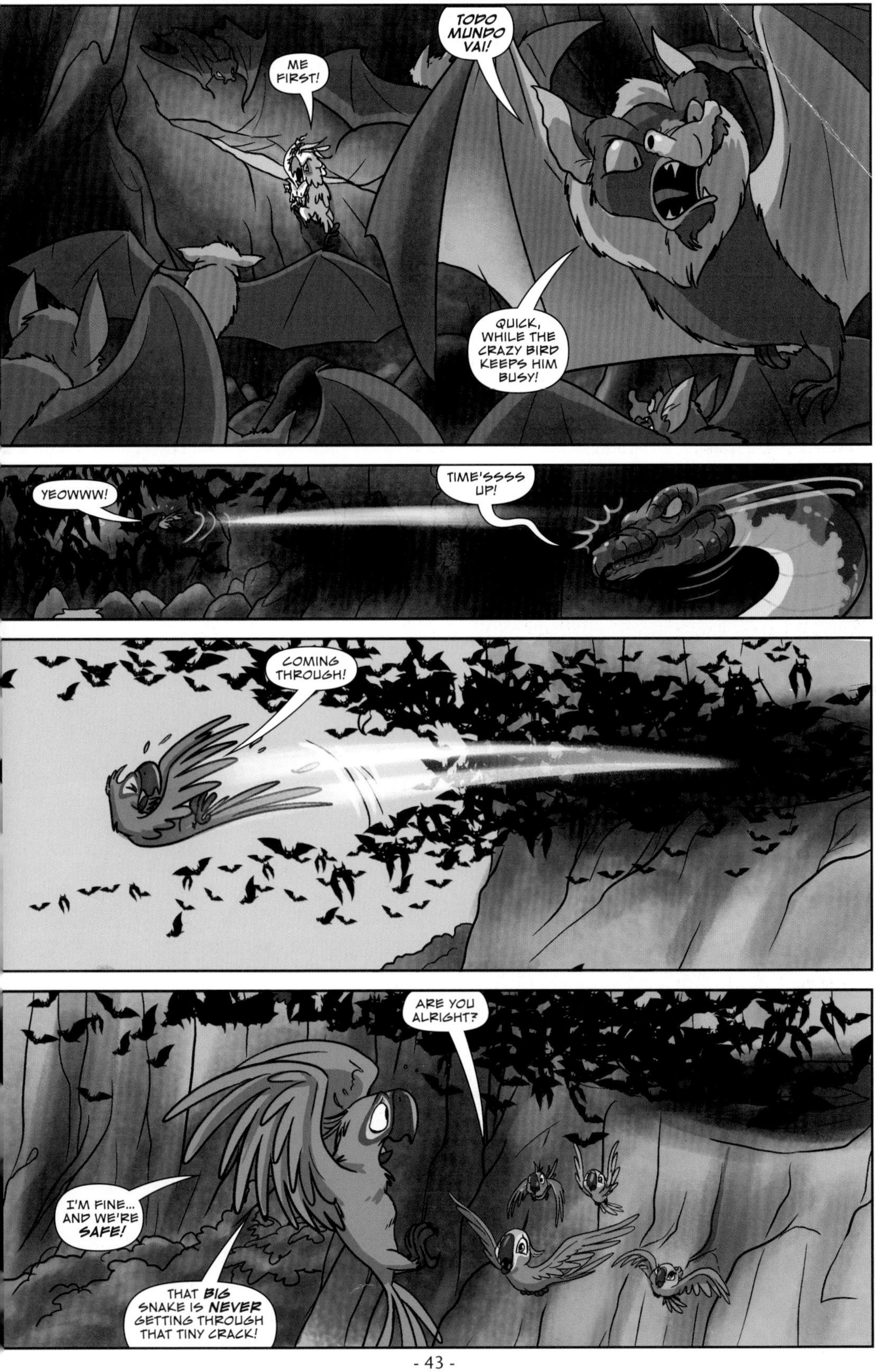
ME FIRST!
TODO MUNDO VAI!
QUICK, WHILE THE CRAZY BIRD KEEPS HIM BUSY!
YEOWWW!
TIME'SSSS UP!
COMING THROUGH!
ARE YOU ALRIGHT?
I'M FINE... AND WE'RE SAFE!
THAT BIG SNAKE IS NEVER GETTING THROUGH THAT TINY CRACK!

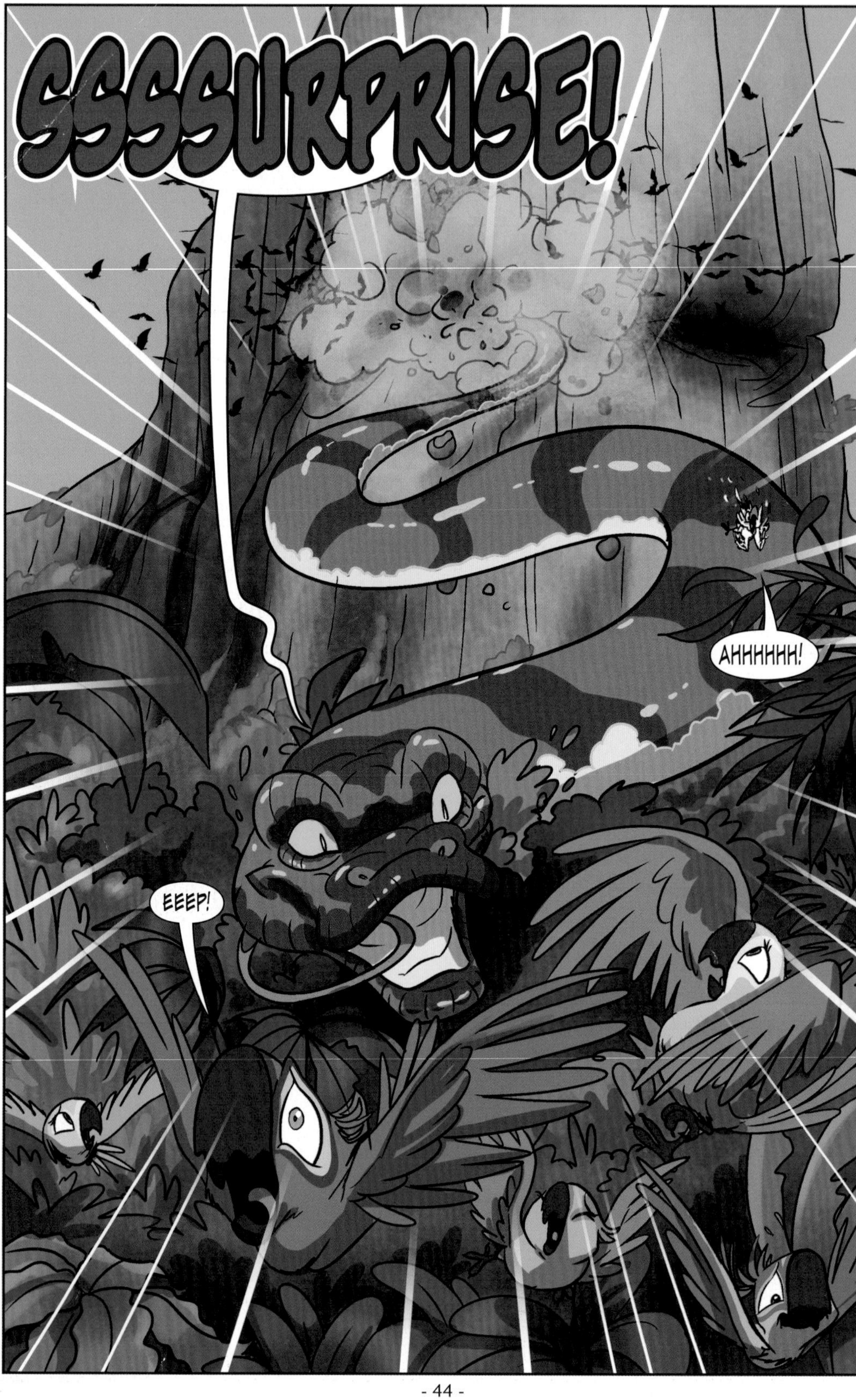
SSSSURPRISE!
AHHHHHH!
EEEP!

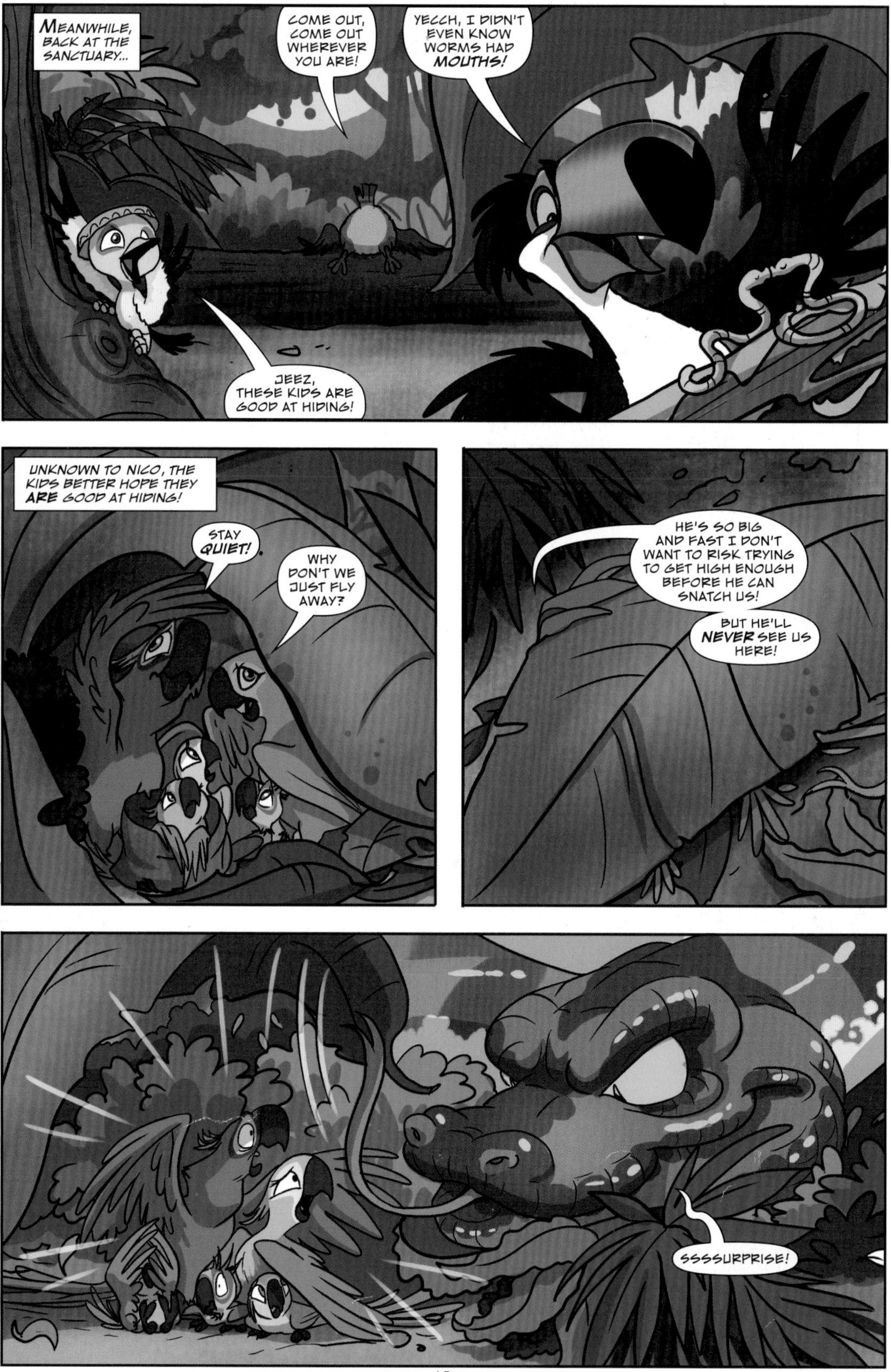
MEANWHILE, BACK AT THE SANCTUARY...
COME OUT, COME OUT WHEREVER YOU ARE!
YECCH, I DIDN'T EVEN KNOW WORMS HAD MOUTHS!
JEEZ, THESE KIDS ARE GOOD AT HIDING!
UNKNOWN TO NICO, THE KIDS BETTER HOPE THEY ARE GOOD AT HIDING!
STAY QUIET!
WHY DON'T WE JUST FLY AWAY?
HE'S SO BIG AND FAST I DON'T WANT TO RISK TRYING TO GET HIGH ENOUGH BEFORE HE CAN SNATCH US!
BUT HE'LL NEVER SEE US HERE!
SSSSURPRISE!

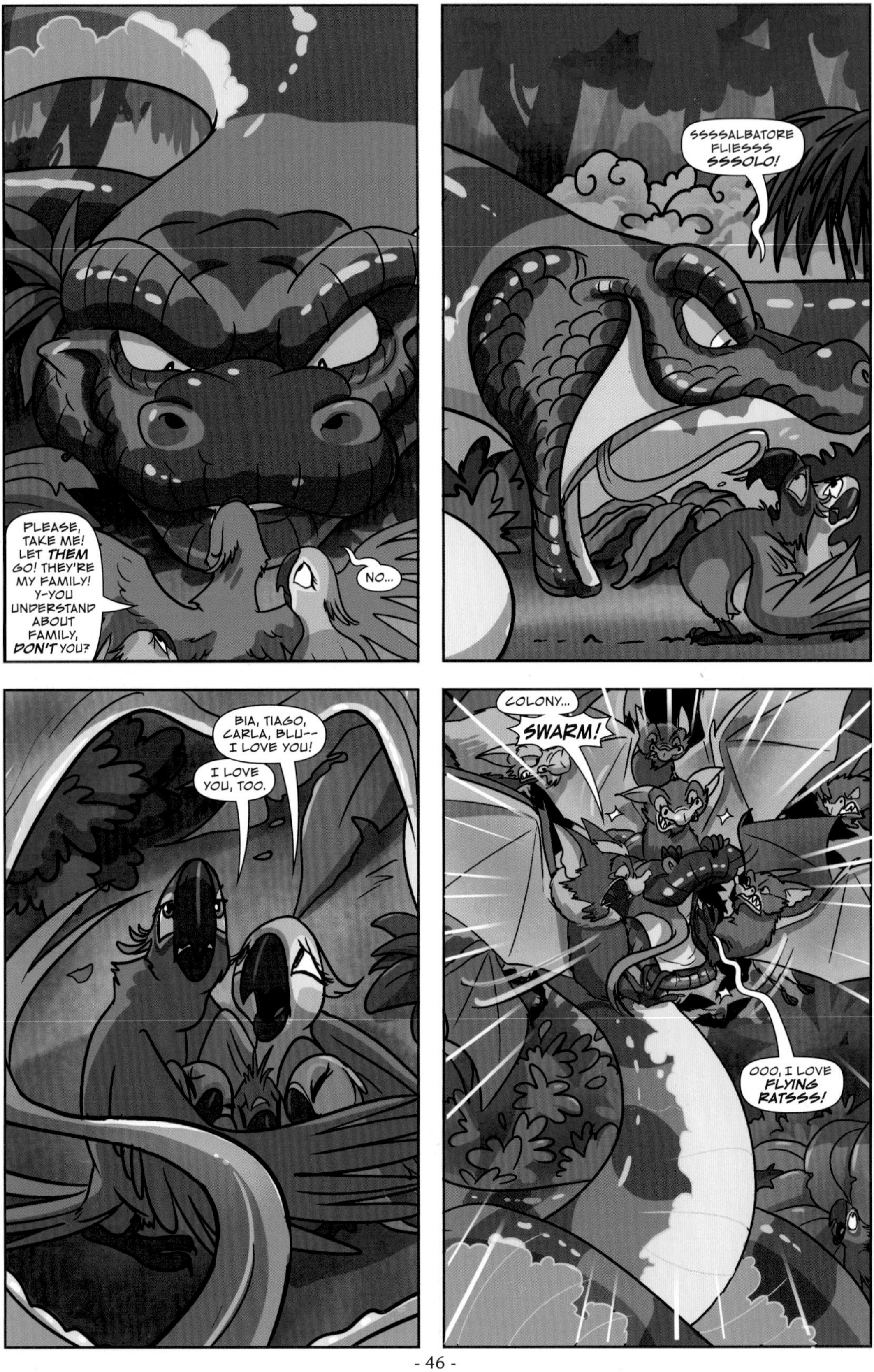
PLEASE, TAKE ME! LET THEM GO! THEY'RE MY FAMILY! Y-YOU UNDERSTAND ABOUT FAMILY, DON'T YOU?
NO...
SSSSALBATORE FLIESSS SSSOLO!
BIA, TIAGO, CARLA, BLU-- I LOVE YOU!
I LOVE YOU, TOO.
COLONY...
SWARM!
OOO, I LOVE FLYING RATSSS!

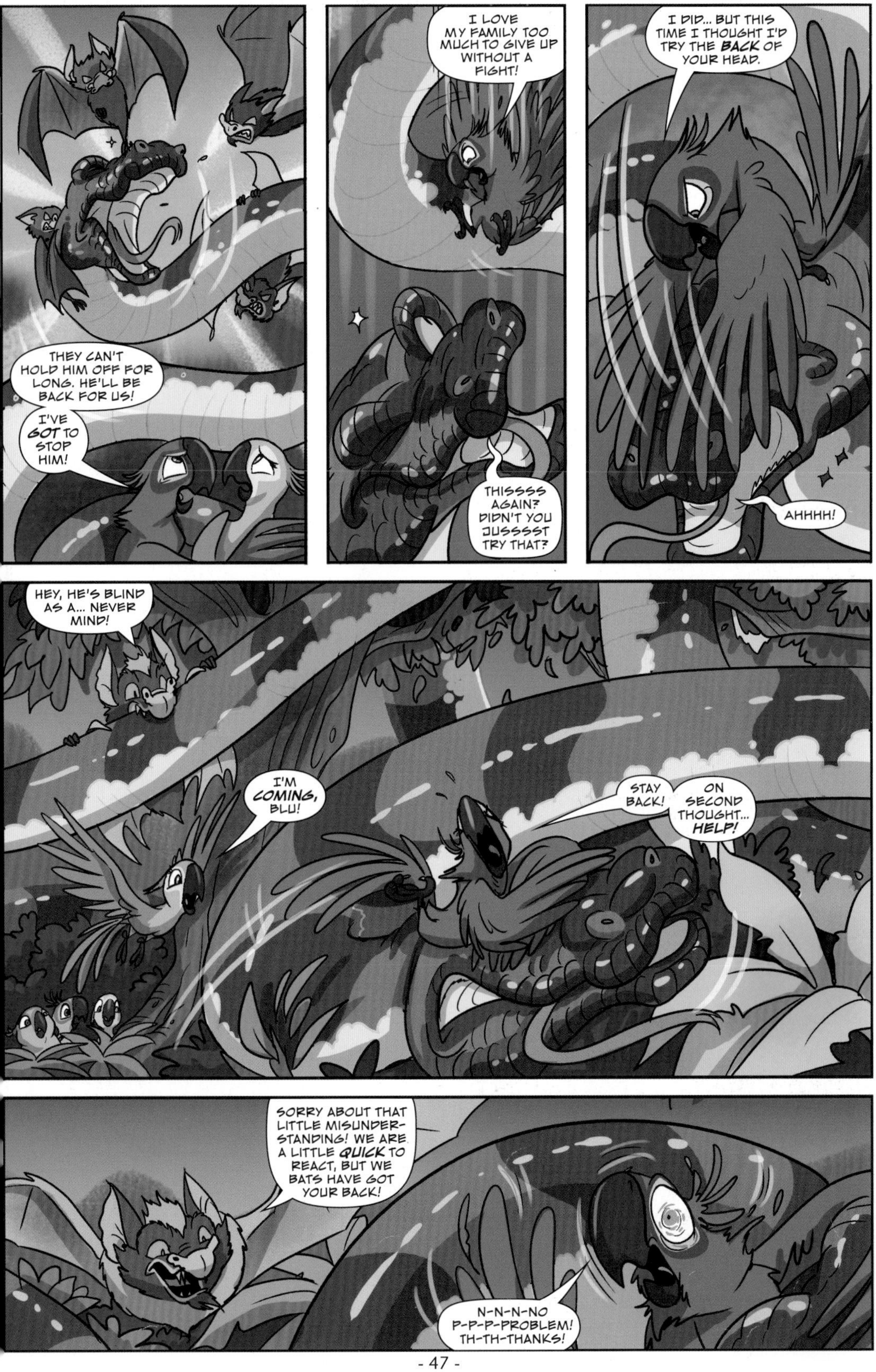
THEY CAN'T HOLD HIM OFF FOR LONG. HE'LL BE BACK FOR US!
I'VE GOT TO STOP HIM!
I LOVE MY FAMILY TOO MUCH TO GIVE UP WITHOUT A FIGHT!
THISSSS AGAIN? DIDN'T YOU JUSSSST TRY THAT?
I DID... BUT THIS TIME I THOUGHT I'D TRY THE BACK OF YOUR HEAD.
AHHHH!
HEY, HE'S BLIND AS A... NEVER MIND!
I'M COMING, BLU!
STAY BACK!
ON SECOND THOUGHT... HELP!
SORRY ABOUT THAT LITTLE MISUNDER-STANDING! WE ARE A LITTLE QUICK TO REACT, BUT WE BATS HAVE GOT YOUR BACK!
N-N-N-NO P-P-P-PROBLEM! TH-TH-THANKS!

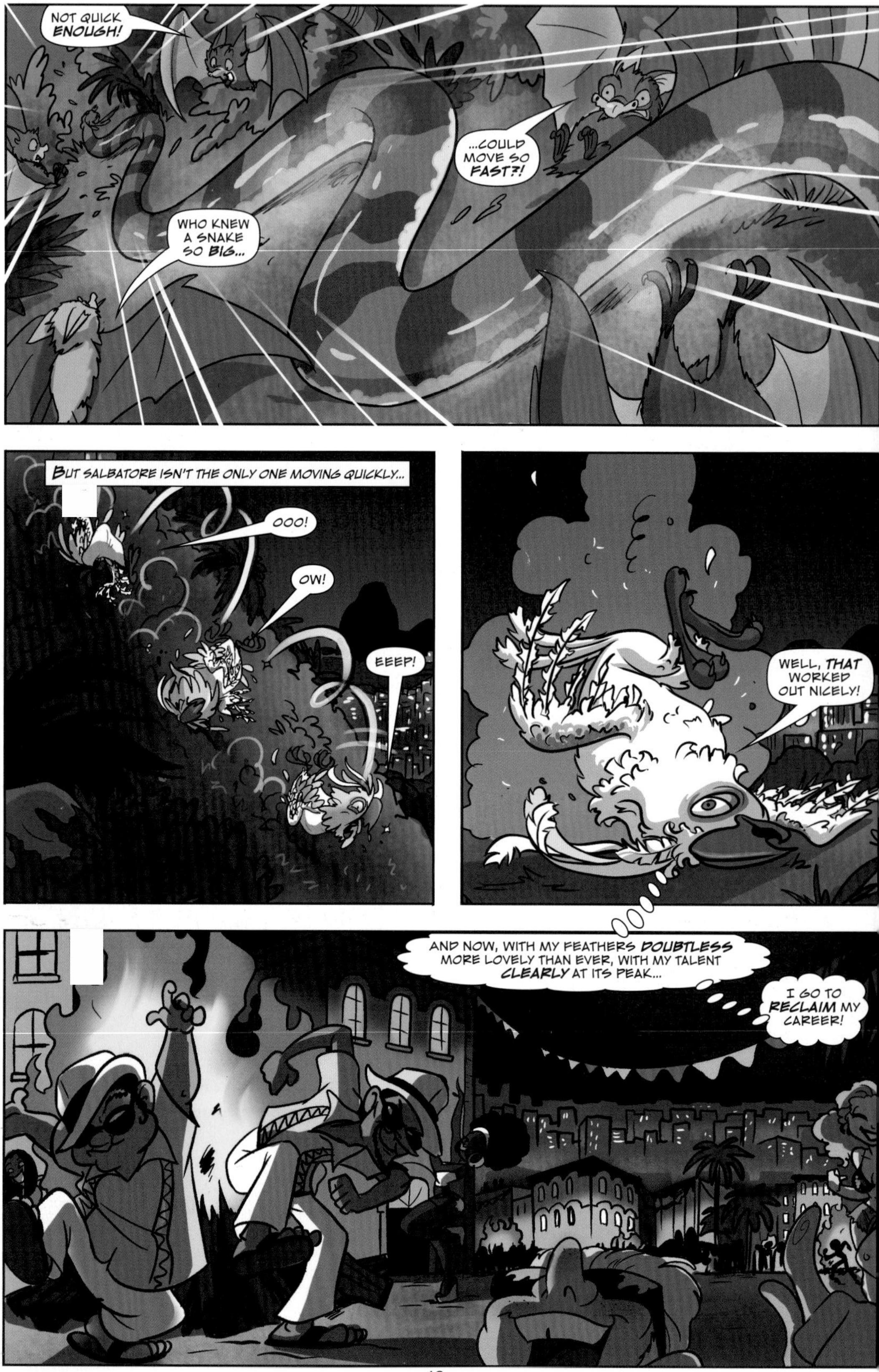

NOT QUICK ENOUGH!
WHO KNEW A SNAKE SO BIG...
...COULD MOVE SO FAST?!
BUT SALBATORE ISN'T THE ONLY ONE MOVING QUICKLY...
OOO!
OW!
EEEP!
WELL, THAT WORKED OUT NICELY!
AND NOW, WITH MY FEATHERS DOUBTLESS MORE LOVELY THAN EVER, WITH MY TALENT CLEARLY AT ITS PEAK...
I GO TO RECLAIM MY CAREER!

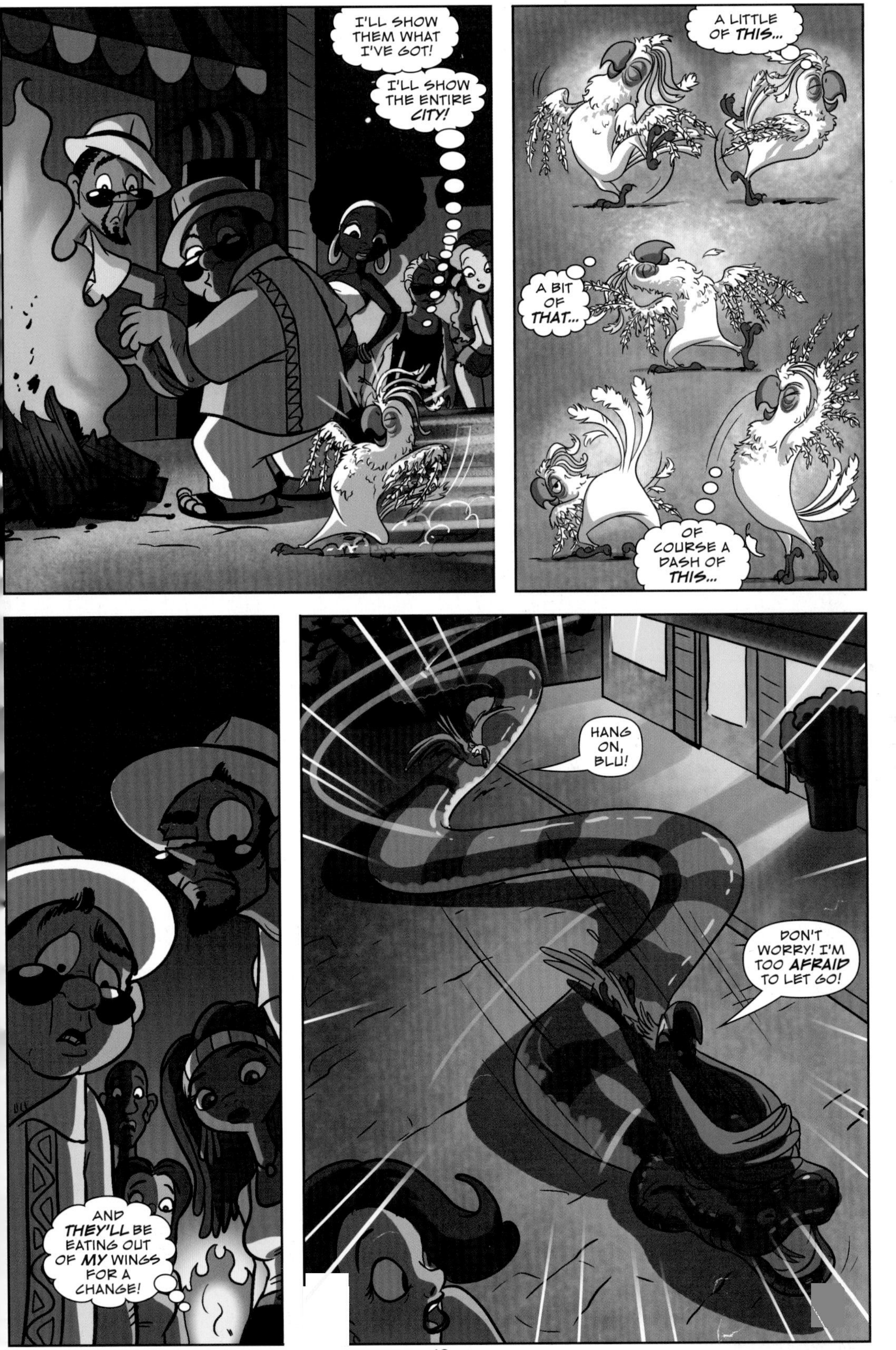
I'LL SHOW THEM WHAT I'VE GOT!
I'LL SHOW THE ENTIRE CITY!
A LITTLE OF THIS...
A BIT OF THAT...
OF COURSE A DASH OF THIS...
AND THEY'LL BE EATING OUT OF MY WINGS FOR A CHANGE!
HANG ON, BLU!
DON'T WORRY! I'M TOO AFRAID TO LET GO!

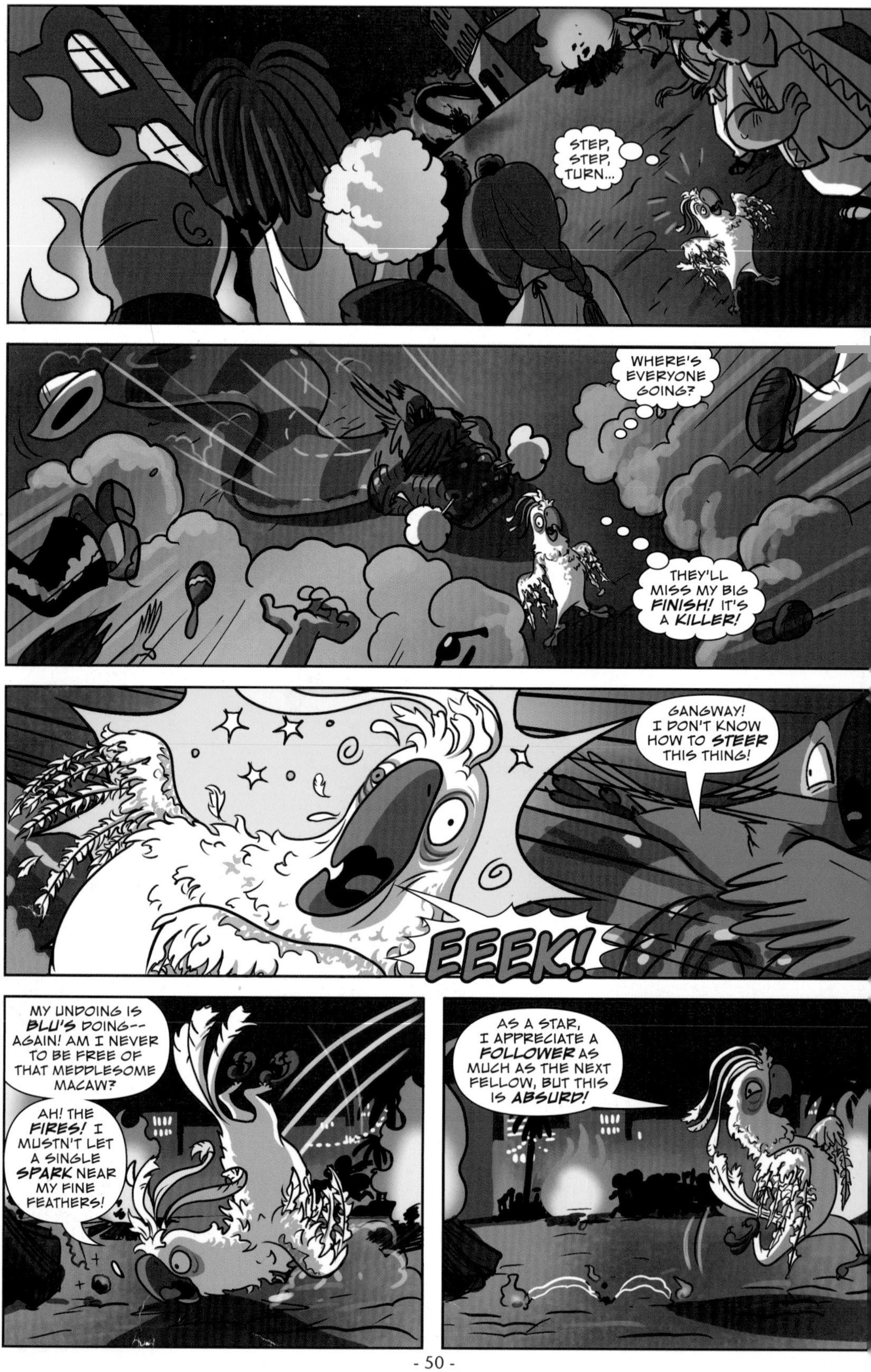
STEP, STEP, TURN...
WHERE'S EVERYONE GOING?
THEY'LL MISS MY BIG FINISH! IT'S A KILLER!
GANGWAY! I DON'T KNOW HOW TO STEER THIS THING!
EEEK!
MY UNDOING IS BLU'S DOING-- AGAIN! AM I NEVER TO BE FREE OF THAT MEDDLESOME MACAW?
AH! THE FIRES! I MUSTN'T LET A SINGLE SPARK NEAR MY FINE FEATHERS!
AS A STAR, I APPRECIATE A FOLLOWER AS MUCH AS THE NEXT FELLOW, BUT THIS IS ABSURD!

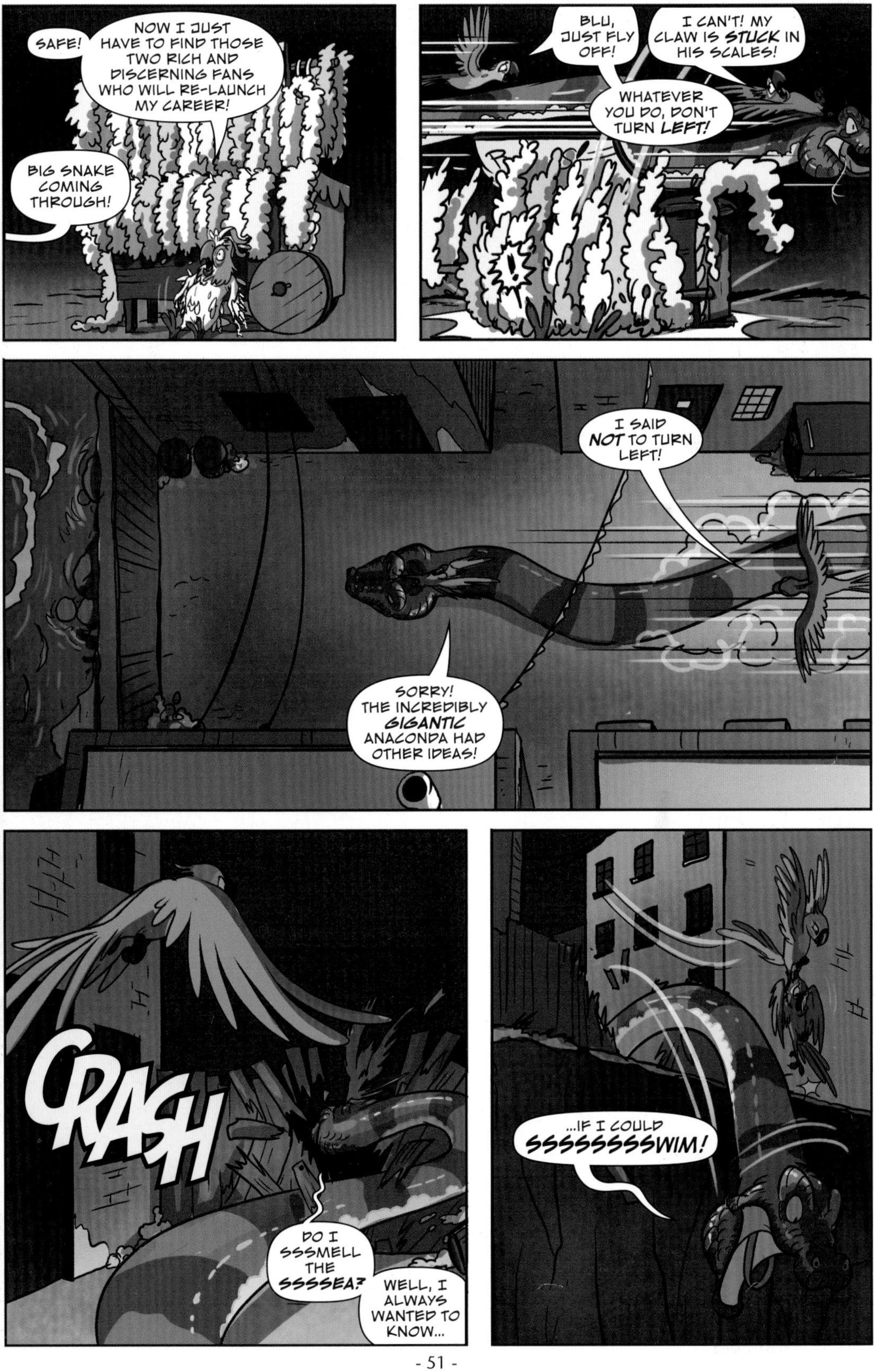
SAFE!
NOW I JUST HAVE TO FIND THOSE TWO RICH AND DISCERNING FANS WHO WILL RE-LAUNCH MY CAREER!
BIG SNAKE COMING THROUGH!
BLU, JUST FLY OFF!
I CAN'T! MY CLAW IS STUCK IN HIS SCALES!
WHATEVER YOU DO, DON'T TURN LEFT!
I SAID NOT TO TURN LEFT!
SORRY! THE INCREDIBLY GIGANTIC ANACONDA HAD OTHER IDEAS!
CRASH
DO I SSSMELL THE SSSSEA?
WELL, I ALWAYS WANTED TO KNOW...
...IF I COULD SSSSSSSSWIM!

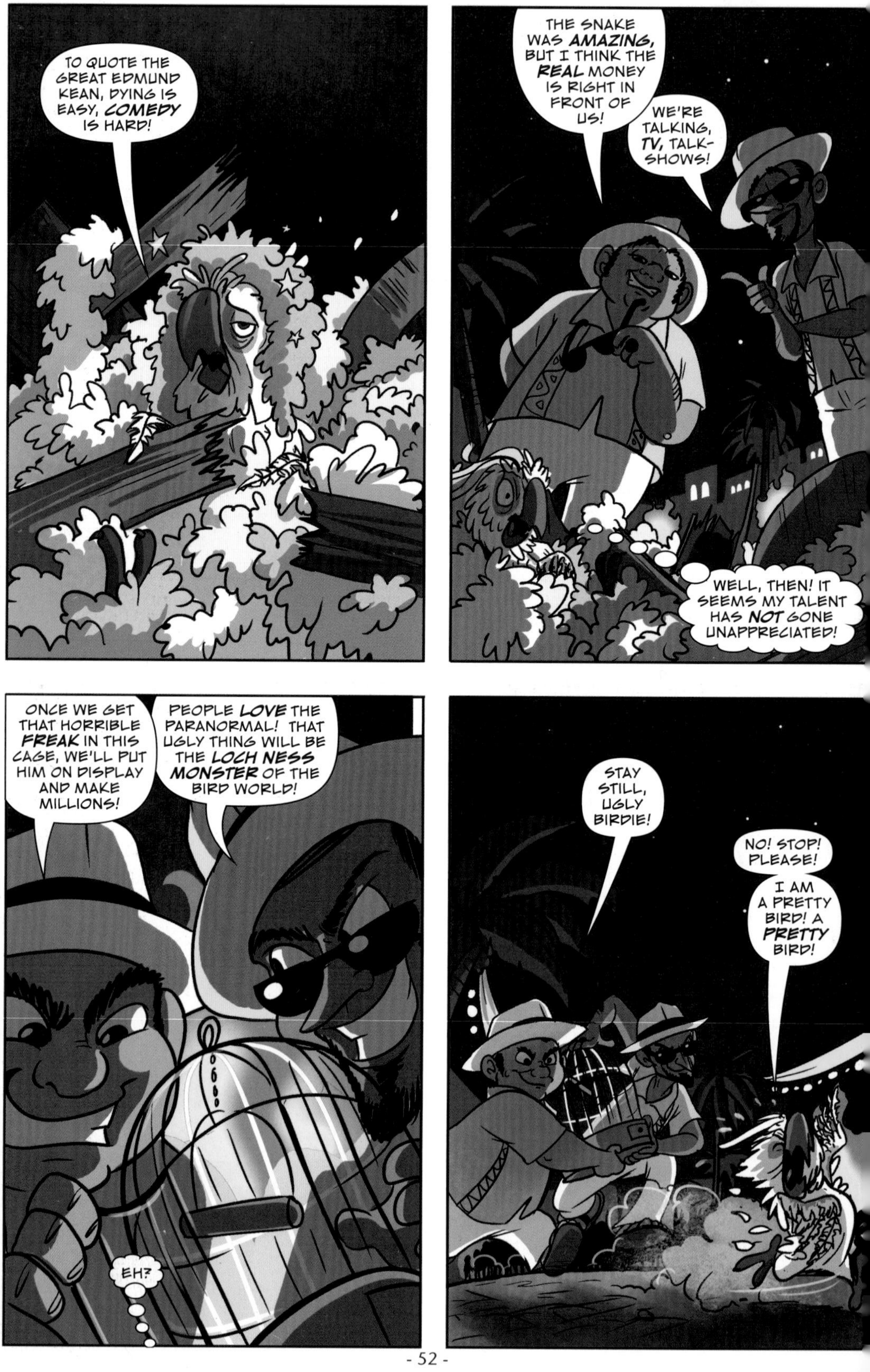
TO QUOTE THE GREAT EDMUND KEAN, DYING IS EASY, COMEDY IS HARD!
THE SNAKE WAS AMAZING, BUT I THINK THE REAL MONEY IS RIGHT IN FRONT OF US!
WE'RE TALKING, TV, TALK-SHOWS!
WELL, THEN! IT SEEMS MY TALENT HAS NOT GONE UNAPPRECIATED!
ONCE WE GET THAT HORRIBLE FREAK IN THIS CAGE, WE'LL PUT HIM ON DISPLAY AND MAKE MILLIONS!
PEOPLE LOVE THE PARANORMAL! THAT UGLY THING WILL BE THE LOCH NESS MONSTER OF THE BIRD WORLD!
EH?
STAY STILL, UGLY BIRDIE!
NO! STOP! PLEASE!
I AM A PRETTY BIRD! A PRETTY BIRD!

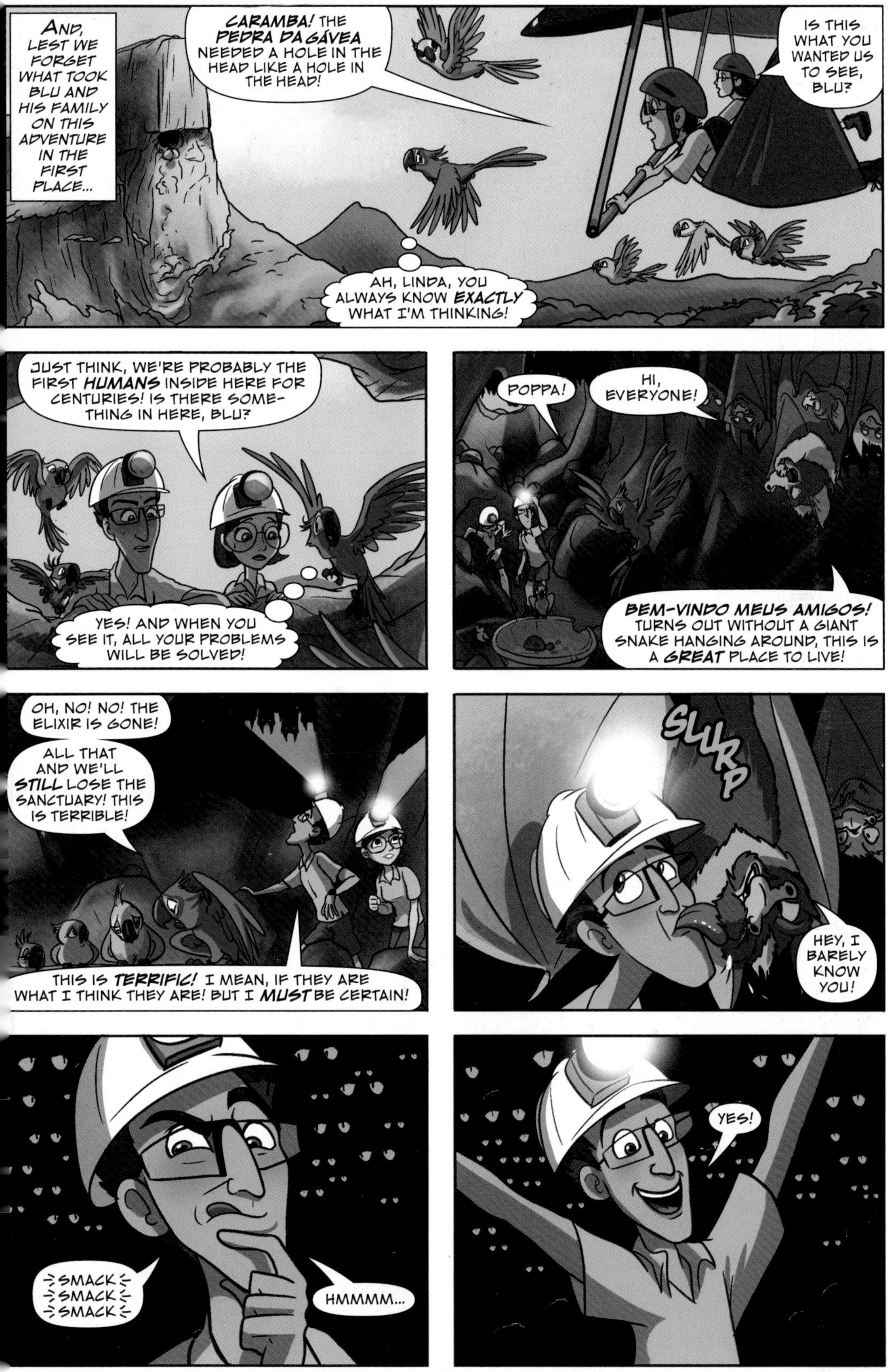
AND, LEST WE FORGET WHAT TOOK BLU AND HIS FAMILY ON THIS ADVENTURE IN THE FIRST PLACE...
CARAMBA! THE PEDRA DA GÁVEA NEEDED A HOLE IN THE HEAD LIKE A HOLE IN THE HEAD!
IS THIS WHAT YOU WANTED US TO SEE, BLU?
AH, LINDA, YOU ALWAYS KNOW EXACTLY WHAT I'M THINKING!
JUST THINK, WE'RE PROBABLY THE FIRST HUMANS INSIDE HERE FOR CENTURIES! IS THERE SOMETHING IN HERE, BLU?
YES! AND WHEN YOU SEE IT, ALL YOUR PROBLEMS WILL BE SOLVED!
POPPA!
HI, EVERYONE!
BEM-VINDO MEUS AMIGOS! TURNS OUT WITHOUT A GIANT SNAKE HANGING AROUND, THIS IS A GREAT PLACE TO LIVE!
OH, NO! NO! THE ELIXIR IS GONE!
ALL THAT AND WE'LL STILL LOSE THE SANCTUARY! THIS IS TERRIBLE!
THIS IS TERRIFIC! I MEAN, IF THEY ARE WHAT I THINK THEY ARE! BUT I MUST BE CERTAIN!
SLURP
HEY, I BARELY KNOW YOU!
SMACK SMACK SMACK
HMMMM...
YES!

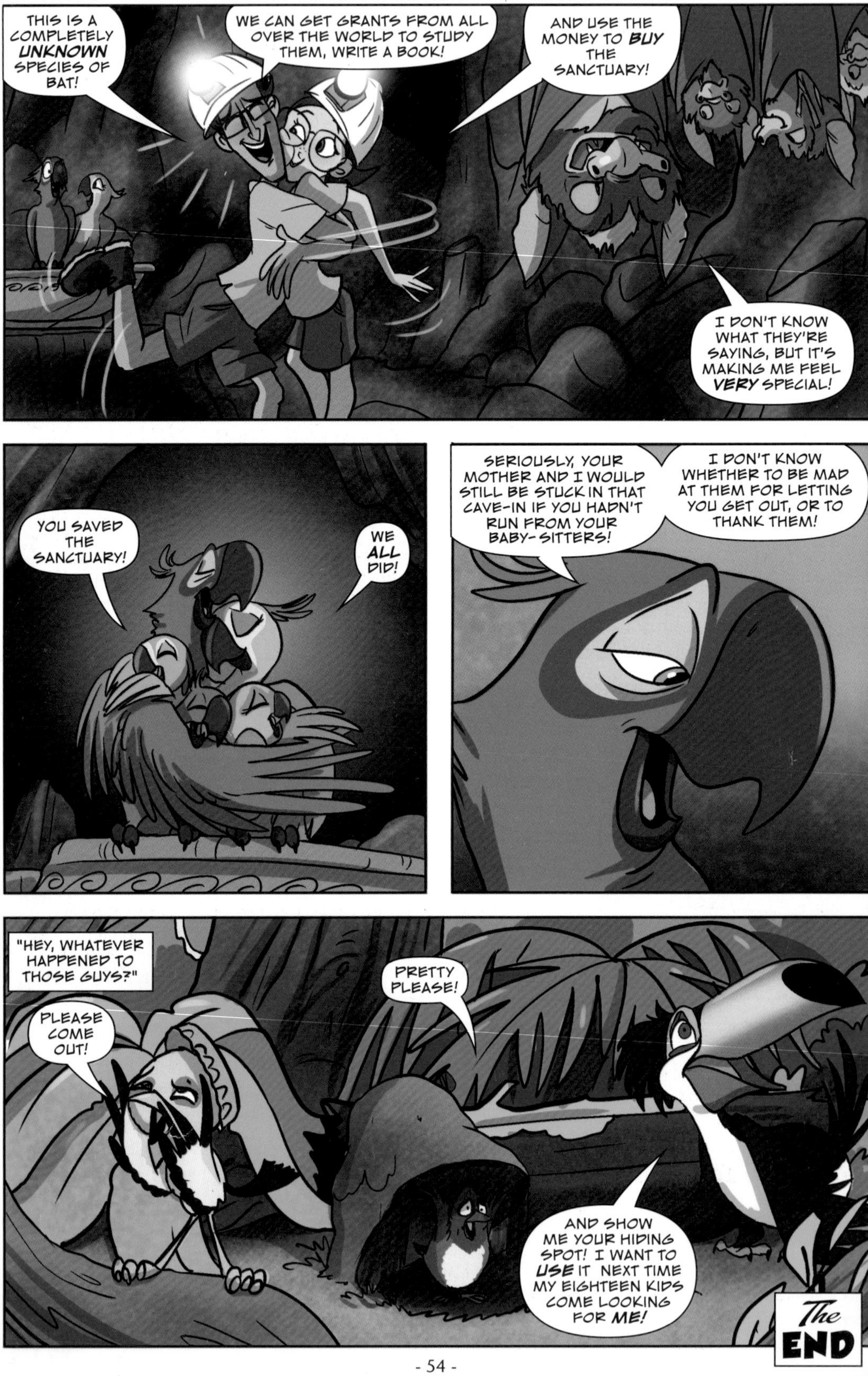
THIS IS A COMPLETELY **UNKNOWN** SPECIES OF BAT!
WE CAN GET GRANTS FROM ALL OVER THE WORLD TO STUDY THEM, WRITE A BOOK!
AND USE THE MONEY TO **BUY** THE SANCTUARY!
I DON'T KNOW WHAT THEY'RE SAYING, BUT IT'S MAKING ME FEEL **VERY** SPECIAL!
YOU SAVED THE SANCTUARY!
WE **ALL** DID!
SERIOUSLY, YOUR MOTHER AND I WOULD STILL BE STUCK IN THAT CAVE-IN IF YOU HADN'T RUN FROM YOUR BABY-SITTERS!
I DON'T KNOW WHETHER TO BE MAD AT THEM FOR LETTING YOU GET OUT, OR TO THANK THEM!
"HEY, WHATEVER HAPPENED TO THOSE GUYS?"
PLEASE COME OUT!
PRETTY PLEASE!
AND SHOW ME YOUR HIDING SPOT! I WANT TO **USE** IT NEXT TIME MY EIGHTEEN KIDS COME LOOKING FOR **ME**!
The END

WATCH OUT FOR PAPERCUTZ™

Welcome to the fine-feathered, first RIO graphic novel from those bird-brains at Papercutz—the flighty folks dedicated to publishing great graphic novels for all ages. I'm Jim Salicrup, the Editor-in-Chief and Designated Luiz-walker. And for those of you paying close attention, we did indeed say "first"! Papercutz is proud to be able to present an all-new, on-going series of graphic novels featuring the high-flying stars of the hit Rio movies. For our premiere offering, we're lucky to have rounded up a trio of top talents:

Photo by Joshua Sugiyama

Stefan Petrucha has written over 20 novels and hundreds of graphic novels. He has appeared on the A&E television series *Paranormal State*, and teaches online classes at the University of Massachusetts. His work has sold over a million copies worldwide. Born in the Bronx, Stefan spent his formative years moving between the big city and the suburbs, both of which made him prefer escapism. A fan of comicbooks, science fiction and horror since learning to read, in high school and college he added a love for all sorts of literary work, eventually learning that the very best fiction always brings you back to reality, so, really, there's no way out. An obsessive compulsion to create his own stories began at age ten and has since taken many forms, including novels, comics and video productions. At times, the need to pay the bills made him a tech writer, an educational writer, a public relations writer and an editor for trade journals, but fiction, in all its forms, has always been his passion. Every year he's made a living at that, he counts a lucky one. Fortunately, there've been many.

James Silvani is a Maui based illustrator and comicbook artist. Born in Laguna Beach, California, he graduated with an art degree from SFSU and dove headfirst into the world of licensed comic and commercial art working on properties such as TMNT, Transformers, Looney Tunes and Animaniacs. After a long stint as a merchandising artist, James returned to graphic storytelling with the relaunch of DARKWING DUCK comicbook series. Currently he is working with Acme Archives providing fine art for Disney and Star Wars.

Amy Mebberson is an Australian comic artist and illustrator. Amy started her career as an inbetweener and assistant animator at Walt Disney Animation Australia, before moving to the USA and beginning a career in comics for Disney, Pixar and the Muppets at Boom! Studios. Her Muppet artwork has also been featured in five storybooks for Little Brown & Co. As an animation artist, Amy worked on *Return to Neverland*, *Cinderella 3*, *Lion King 1.5* and *An Extremely Goofy Movie* at Walt Disney Animation Australia. Amy currently draws MY LITTLE PONY comics for IDW publishing as well as her Disney Fine art with Acme Archives and other art projects for the Walt Disney Company and other licensors. Amy also writes and draws the internet Disney fan-comic "Pocket Princesses." Amy lives in Southern California and spends too much time at Disneyland.

We're as happy as can be with how our first graphic novel has turned out, and we're eager to find out what you thought of it. So please, send us your feedback to our very first RIO graphic novel. And coming soon, our second RIO graphic novel, "The Creature from Blu's Lagoon."

Thanks, Jim

STAY IN TOUCH!

EMAIL: salicrup@papercutz.com
WEB: papercutz.com
TWITTER: @papercutzgn
FACEBOOK: PAPERCUTZGRAPHICNOVELS
FANMAIL: Papercutz, 160 Broadway, Suite 700, East Wing, New York, NY 10038

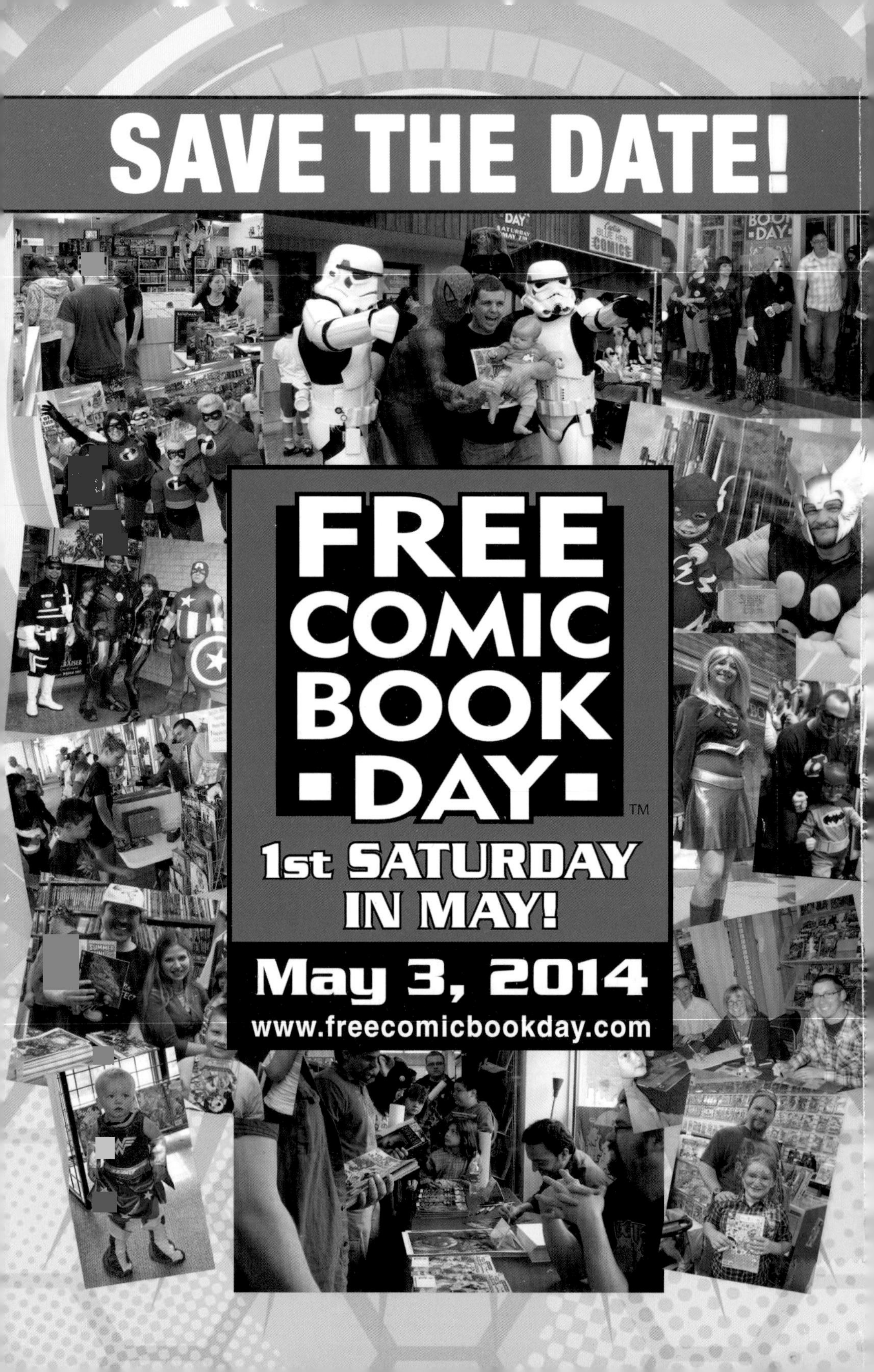
SAVE THE DATE!
FREE COMIC BOOK DAY™
1st SATURDAY IN MAY!
May 3, 2014
www.freecomicbookday.com